TWO THRILLERS

GIORGOS MANIOTIS

Two Thrillers

Translation
NICHOLAS KOSTIS

KEDROS

Typeset in Greece
by Photokyttaro Ltd.
14, Armodiou St., Athens 105 52
Tel. 32.44.111
and printed by
M. Monteverdis & P. Alexopoulos
Metamorphosis, Athens
For
Kedros Publishers, S.A.,
3, G. Gennadiou St., Athens 106 78,
Tel. 38.09.712 – Fax 38.31.981
June 1996

The two stories in this volume are
selected from Repertório tis Ánixis
Cover design by Dimitris Kalokyris

ISBN 960-04-1197-2

WHAT DID THE BLACKBIRD HEAR?

DORA AND TAKIS HAD JUST GOTTEN MARRIED. After spending their wedding night unceremoniously in one of the hotels in the center of town, the next day at daybreak they got into their car, put their suitcases in the back seat, attached two tiny sacks containing wedding sugared almonds to the rear-view mirror over the windshield and, full of laughter and joy, set out for a marvelous inn high up in the mountains that only Takis knew. The road was all curves and jagged red boulders and they drove through dark forests with towering trees and small lakes.

For some time now they had not encountered another car. Behind the wheel Takis was humming happily. —Just where was he taking her, Dora wondered. She had never before been in these parts. —He was taking her to the most erotic hotel in the world. —Fine, said Dora, but the place did seem a bit desolate! —Why did she need people

9

when they had each other! — That was, of course, a big consolation, but would he please explain to her why he was driving like a madman? — He was in a hurry to get there with her; he could hardly wait! — If that was the reason then he was right to step on it, Dora said, smiling naughtily. — But why was she so nervous and restless? — She was neither nervous nor restless, she was simply getting dizzy driving fast the way he was round the curves. — His dream had finally become a reality, Takis said, changing the subject. — Did he mean their wedding? — Yes, that's what he meant! — They really and truly were living in bliss since last night when they were married, Dora concurred and stretched languorously.

"Dora, I want to ask you something very delicate," Takis said in the midst of humming the same song over and over. — He could ask her anything he liked. — Was it true that she had not been with another man? — Tonight when their honeymoon began officially, he would find out for himself. Her answer convinced Takis that she had not been with another man, and for the moment he felt infinitely happy, so much so that he nearly ran the car off the road. — What in heaven's name was he doing, why wasn't he more careful? He was going to land them in some ravine. — Never in his wildest dreams had he imagined that Dora, his great love, would finally consent to marry him. — He was young, handsome, had a good job, why shouldn't she marry him? Dora joked. — He was happy, very happy, Takis exclaimed and stopped the car in the middle of the road under the shade of an old plane tree. — Why had he stopped so abruptly? Takis let go of the steering wheel and grabbed Dora. "Kiss me!" he said, struggling to find her lips. Dora attempted to bring him back to order by assuming a mincing manner. — What a naughty boy he was, how impetuous he was. He must learn to control himself. What he wanted could not possibly be done there, in the middle of the road, in broad daylight!

Suddenly Dora saw a black object on the windshield and was frightened. "What's that?" she asked, pointing at something behind the window. Takis pulled away and, all hot and bothered the way he was, tried to concentrate in order to understand what had so attracted the attention of his sweet little wife. There was something out there on the hood of the car. In fact, a blackbird had alighted on it! — How did that blackbird happen to be there? Dora asked and realized she was trembling. It was a robust, well-nourished bird with glossy, black plumage and a dark orange yellow bill. It was one of those blackbirds that speak like parrots. Cruel, arrogant birds that feed on small pieces of flesh. "Get out so we can catch it!" Dora said, and opened the car door.

IT WAS NEARLY NOON. They had stopped in the middle of the road, climbed out of the car and were observing, as if magnetized, the blackbird that quite unexpectedly had alighted on the hood of their car. Dora had begun to feel a strange tenderness for this poor creature. Fortunately it did not appear to be wounded. "It's probably just dizzy," said Takis, "it looks as if it was in a cage and is still numb." Dora reached out with her hand and touched it.

"Look," she said to her companion, "it's letting me touch it!" A few moments later Takis also grew courageous and caressed its head with his finger. It truly was a beautiful bird; its wings were as black as ebony. Dora picked it up gently with her two hands and folded it in her arms with endless tenderness, just as she would have done with a small child. Suddenly the bird began to talk in a loud, hoarse voice, as if its beak and throat were full of broken and crushed glass.

"Help! Help! He's murdering me! Help! Don't strangle me! Don't strangle me! Mercy! Mercy! Help!" the blackbird screamed, then settled down in the warmth of Dora's arms. Takis, who hadn't realized that it was the bird talking, looked around in terror to determine where this harsh sound was coming from. Nor had Dora realized who was screaming and she thought that someone near them was calling for help. The blackbird, however, started screaming again, "Help! Help! He's strangling me! He's strangling me! I don't want to die! I don't want to die!" Dora looked at the bird with amazement. — That's who was screaming! — Unquestionably it was the bird that was talking, seeing as it was a myna bird, Takis concluded none too soon. Dora looked around at the landscape and was seized by an unexplainable terror. She told her companion that she was frightened and climbed back into the car with the blackbird in her arms. — They should leave that dreadful place at once; she had a bad premonition.

"Just what do you think you're doing?" Takis asked, surprised. "Are you taking the bird with you?" — Naturally she was taking it with her. This bird was their good luck.

INSIDE THE AUTOMOBILE, NO ONE SPOKE. Takis drove immersed in thought and Dora stared straight ahead at the road which seemed to never end. Suddenly the blackbird started shrieking again, "Help! Help! He's strangling me! Help! I don't want to die! Help!" What a strange bird, Takis thought; it keeps repeating the same phrase.

"Do you think it witnessed a murder?" Dora asked.

"Of course not, it's probably repeating something it heard on television," Takis reassured her.

"Help! Help! He's strangling me! Help! I don't want to die!" Its voice was so alive and anguished that Dora was certain the bird had witnessed a real murder. — How could she be so certain? — Because if it had seen the murder on television, it would not have remembered it all that well. In time it would have forgotten it, the way we forget lots of things that we see on television. The murder, however, in some strange way had become an obsession with this bird. This meant that it had experienced the actual event. — There was no way in the world that Takis could accept her explanation! — And why, might she ask, couldn't he accept it? — All right, that was one interpretation, Takis said condescendingly, anxious to drop the subject. "Help! Help! Aaaah! Help! He's choking me! Aaaah!" the blackbird started screaming again quite unexpectedly, looking now at one, now at the other with its orange eyes.

THE SMALL, ALL-WHITE INN STOOD SILENTLY in a clearing of the forest. In front of it was an enormous yard covered with asphalt for the guests to park their cars. All the windows were shut and the place looked deserted. If you observed more carefully, however, you would notice that the yard had been carefully swept and that the surrounding shrubs had been meticulously trimmed. There wasn't a dilapidated window or a broken roof tile anywhere in sight — nothing, that is, to suggest that a mood of desolation had installed itself in this small, picturesque inn. Except that a strange silence prevailed everywhere around, as if life had stopped. Perhaps this was due to the hour; it was late afternoon and the surrounding trees had started to turn mauve with the gradual arrival of twilight. Takis and Dora's car had come to a halt before the main entrance with the large lantern.

—So this was the marvelous inn? Dora asked herself. —This was it! Takis replied brusquely. "But the place is deserted, love! At least it looks that way to me," Dora said and to prove her point she began to blow the horn furiously. The sound of the horn in this wilderness with the dark, silent fir trees all around, the white inn standing there all shut up and silent, and the darkening sky slowly blending with the asphalt of the yard paralyzed Dora. Fortunately she was still holding the warm bird in her arms. "I'm afraid, Takis!" she stammered through her teeth.

"What are you afraid of, love?" Takis replied, and he went on blowing the horn in the same lively manner as his wife had done a few moments earlier.

15

"There's no one here, we'd better leave!" Dora insisted. But Takis would not give in that easily and was now blowing the horn in a rage.

"What in hell's going on?" he kept saying to himself. "Are they dead? They can't be!" The heavy, wooden door opened slowly. A warm, orange light, full of snugness and sweetness, came pouring out. An elderly woman with gray hair and a face nearly petrified by solitude appeared at the entrance. She was impeccably groomed and was wearing a gray, elegant dress with a thin leather belt around her waist, two pearl earrings and a blue shawl thrown over her shoulders. Dora was the first to see her.

"Look, Takis, a woman!" she said to her companion, her heart transfixed by a strange uneasiness. Takis leaned over in her direction to see what she looked like. —Good, it was the innkeeper's wife; time for them to get out.

"Good evening," the woman said to them as she slowly approached their car.

"Have you any rooms?" Takis asked.

"Many!" the old lady replied with a touch of sadness in her voice. —Good, they'd like her to prepare the best room she had for them. —Were they planning to stay long? At least ten days! "Very well!" the woman said and started to open the back door of the car to take out one of the suitcases.

"Is your husband still alive?" asked Takis, who in the meantime had climbed out of the car. The

16

woman drew herself up and looked at him strangely. — Of course he was still alive! What sort of question was that? To set her mind at rest Takis told her that he often used to stay at their inn a long time ago.

"I don't remember you!" the woman replied and bent over again to take one of the suitcases in the back seat of the car.

"How's your son?" Takis asked out of the blue as he grabbed hold of a suitcase through the other door. The woman appeared startled by the question, but as before she tried not to show it. — Their son had grown up and left home. He was now living alone in the city, the old lady informed Takis while holding the suitcase with her hand and looking into his eyes. As Dora put out her foot to climb out of the car, the blackbird began to scream:

"Help! Help! He's strangling me! Help! I don't want to die! Help!"

"What's that?" the old lady asked, terrorized and realizing only too well that it was good-bye to her glorious and genteel serenity for the next ten days. Dora explained that it was her bird and that ever since it had witnessed a murder on television the wretched creature was constantly reenacting the scene. The woman did not believe a word of what Dora said. "A murder on television?" she muttered, and smiled wearily and enigmatically. "I'll go and prepare your room!" she announced and disappeared inside the inn with the suitcase, leaving the door behind her wide open.

THE ROOM WAS IMMENSE, WITH ALL-WHITE WALLS. The furniture, bed and wardrobes consisted of heavy, walnut pieces—the sort of thing that in the past noble families used to have custom-made to last for a lifetime. Everything glittered and gleamed with cleanliness and love. Sparkling white sheets and dark red, soft blankets. They had just stepped into their room. Behind them, an elderly gentleman dressed in a dark blue valet's suit was carrying their suitcases. "This is where you'll stay!" he said as he attempted to put the suitcases down on the floor without doing any damage. Dora noticed the effort he was making and told her husband, who was standing there with his mouth open, to lend him a hand. Takis immediately offered to help, but the innkeeper had already arranged the suitcases in a corner. To somehow make amends, Takis took out some money to tip him. The innkeeper, however, refused. "The bill at the end!" he said. Afraid that he would only insult him by insisting further, Takis shrank back abashed. His former acquaintance was such a venerable old man. His body had remained the same, youthful and upright; only his face showed traces of the years that had passed. It was as if old age had slowly started to efface his features with a magic sponge. And over this silent destruction lay the gray ashes of solitude and the burden of the impending end that was so visible. "The bill at the end!" the old innkeeper repeated wearily, then went on to say, "if you want to enjoy the view in the morning, you can open the window at the back. It's worth the effort!" — Was the sea really visible from that window? the young bride asked, full of joy and hope. — No, he replied, the only thing visible was a dark ravine.

The innkeeper then shuffled over to a closed door, opened it and showed them the bathroom. Takis took a look inside and was delighted; it was the same as before — spacious and spotlessly clean. — If they should need anything at all, the innkeeper continued, they merely had to pull the white cord above their bed; a bell would then ring and they would hear it. Dora, who thought the innkeeper was dawdling in their room on purpose, reminded Takis to give the man something. Takis, whose mind was somewhat muddled, put his hand in his pocket and again took out a paper bill. "I said the bill at the end!" the innkeeper again cut him off. Takis was mortified and tried to talk about something else. — He really didn't remember him at all? The old innkeeper lifted his head and looked into his eyes. — No, no matter how hard he tried, he couldn't place his face. — It had, of course, been

19

at least ten years, but he often used to stay at their inn in the past. — How could he possibly remember him? Ten years ago lots of people used to stay in their small inn. — It was true, in the past loads of people used to stay there, said Takis, who was puzzled by the present desolation. The old innkeeper smiled bitterly. — They had grown old and the guests had grown tired of them, he replied and turned his back to them to go out. Before he closed the door behind him, the blackbird began to screech:

"Help! Help! I don't want to die! I don't want to die! He's strangling me! He's strangling me! Help! Help!"

He turned around for an instant, looked at it and said "Ssh!" while shaking his finger at it, and then went out of the room, closing the door softly behind him. Dora and Takis, standing motionless beside the bed, looked at each other with anguish and fear.

IN ABOUT AN HOUR THEIR ROOM WAS IN CHAOS. Dora and Takis had opened their suitcases and were trying to get ready for the supper downstairs to which they had been invited by the two hospitable innkeepers. Various objects were strewn all over the room. — Well, did she like it here? Takis asked Dora from the bathroom while shaving. — She liked it all right, but she was afraid, Dora replied from in front of the mirror as she tried to attach a false eyelash to her left eye. — What was she afraid of? he asked. — How could he be so insensitive? Couldn't he tell from the general atmosphere that something evil had happened at this inn? — Perhaps she felt that they should pack their bags and leave? — No, of course not, not now that they had unpacked and gotten settled. He should have spoken sooner. — Then what in blazes was wrong with her and why was she complaining? — Even she couldn't explain what the matter was, but her intuition told her that they were in danger in this house. — Why didn't she tell him what exactly was going on in her head? Dora, who had finished adjusting the two false eyelashes, moved away from the mirror and approached the bathroom door. — She was sure those two old people had murdered someone, she said to Takis who was still shaving, and — it was quite obvious to her — they and the bird were the sole witnesses. — His wife had too much imagination. — Her instinct was never wrong. He would see, in the last analysis she was the one who would have been right. — What did she think those two old people were about to do? — Couldn't he see for himself that the inn was practically deserted? — He agreed that she was right about that. — They had taken them in as guests so as to have plenty of time to do away with

21

them at their leisure. — In that case, they would be wise to pack their bags and clear out, Takis asserted while applying some cologne to his face. — No, nothing could make them leave that place because his little wife Dora, in addition to her imagination, was very obstinate. They would stay at the inn and get to the bottom of the mystery no matter what. — They would do exactly as she wanted, Takis agreed while looking at a small cut from the razor on his face. The blackbird, which all this time had been observing the scene while clutching the shower hose, began to screech, "I want to live! Help! He's strangling me! He's strangling me! I want to live! I want to live!"

TAKIS PUT ON A DARK BLUE SUIT OF FINE WOOL and Dora a beautiful evening dress that shimmered and glittered. When they went downstairs and entered the large parlor of the inn they could hardly believe their eyes. Near the hearth where the fire was crackling, a table spread with candlesticks, crystal glasses, expensive porcelain dishes and heavy silver placeware awaited them. The tablecloth was a work of art, embroidered entirely by hand, with thousands of flowers and small birds — a barely perceptible nature quivering and caught on the delicate, dainty lace. From the refined smells diffused throughout the room they realized right away that the meal about to follow would be truly unforgettable. "My wife has cooked specially for you!" the innkeeper informed them. Dora and Takis did not know how to thank them enough. — She hadn't cooked for years, the innkeeper continued. — What an honor! It was a table fit for a king, said Dora, bedazzled. She had approached and was examining the crystal and porcelain nearly in a state of enchantment. — The food had already been served, they should sit down before everything got cold. It would be a shame to eat it cold, the old lady announced sweetly. — They would sit down with pleasure, but why were there only two chairs around the table, Takis inquired? — It wasn't proper for the innkeepers to eat with the guests. Besides, they were old and the food was a little too heavy for them. Ordinarily they didn't eat at night. Dora, however, was unyielding and insisted that they also sit down at the table. — It wasn't right for them to be eating while the others watched from a distance. Furthermore they had no more secrets to tell one another, they had declared their love again and again, more than a thousand times, a little company would do them good. The two old people accepted their invitation with alacrity, pulled up two chairs, added two more place settings with all the essentials and also sat down at the table. The innkeeper opened a bottle of dark red wine and started filling their glasses. He had made it himself when he was a young man and had been saving it in his cellar for more than twenty years. Takis, unable to restrain himself, took a sip. — It was positively exquisite wine. Dora followed his example. — It certainly was; she couldn't recall ever having drunk anything like it in her life. The old lady had already sat down and was waiting for them to finish with all these preliminaries. After the innkeeper had filled the glasses, Takis decided that the moment had come for them to start eating all these marvelous things that smelled so good. The old lady, who all this time had been looking at them in silence, was of another opinion. Before they started striking their knives and forks, it might not be such a bad idea if they said a little prayer. They all welcomed her proposal enthusiastically, because they were not exactly atheistical. It was simply that the era, with its haste, made them forget their religious obligations. They crossed their hands and placed them on the tablecloth, in front of the dishes. The old lady began the prayer in a tranquil and sweet voice:

"We thank the Lord our God for granting us one more day of health and happiness, we thank him also for sending us two young people for company, and finally we thank him for this table with all these good things which he has provided. Amen!"

"There," she said when she had finished, and

she immediately began to serve the food. Dora, who had kept her eyes downcast throughout the prayer, had observed that in the very center of the dishes were drawings of fearsome hunting scenes, with dying animals and hunters galloping proudly to the slaughter on flaming horses, while brandishing their swords and javelins. Takis had begun to eat. — The food was indeed out of this world. Dora also decided to take her first forkful. — Yes, it was excellent, only she had no idea what she was eating. It had plums and almonds in it, of course, but she wasn't able to determine what kind of meat it was. The old lady refused to tell her. — She couldn't do that, it was one of her secrets. Takis, for someone so elegantly dressed, was devouring the food with astonishing gluttony. He remembered from the past that the old lady was a fantastic cook and this had added to his appetite. "I was many things, but now I'm not!" the genteel old lady murmured softly as she brought the glass of wine to her lips. The innkeeper thought that it was time for them to clink glasses.

"To our health!" the others repeated and raised their glasses. They wanted to clink glasses, but the distances around the enormous table were too remote and they didn't feel like moving. Besides, it would have been excessive. So they contented themselves with simply raising their glasses and saluting one another from their seats.

"Are these two really married?" the old lady asked her husband unsuspectingly and very ingenuously. — What a treacherous question, thought Dora. Of course they were married, they had gotten married last night. — They had only been married for a day, Takis added trying to make light of the situation. The old woman's eyes filled with tears. She was deeply moved. — Tomorrow morning she would make a cake for them. And the innkeeper would open a bottle of wine that he had intended to open at his son's wedding. "Did you marry for love?" the old lady came right back with another, darker question. Takis, to prevent the mood from becoming somber, decided to play the buffoon whose mouth is stuffed with food and who is so naive and thick-skinned that he doesn't grasp the verbal thrusts.

"For love, for love!" he assured her as he picked clean a tasty little wing dipped in a divine sauce.

"The two of us also married for love centuries ago," she informed him, nodding at her husband.

"We were happy, we can't complain!" muttered the old man, somewhat sleepy from the heavy food and the wine.

"Yes, up until a certain point we were happy," the old lady nearly stammered, trying to conceal her emotion.

But Dora, who was just waiting for the opportunity to get back at her, asked quite spontaneously while smiling naively and cheerfully, "and then?" The woman did not reply. The innkeeper, however, did reply as he undid two of the large buttons on his uniform that were close to his neck.

"Then we got into a rut!" he said and dropped his head.

"That was later!" the old lady said softly.

Dora felt as if she had been given the coup de grâce and wanted to dispel the atmosphere of grief and nostalgia crushing them. —It was a fabulous meal. Would the old lady give her the recipe? —She would give it to her when they left. "In other words, never!" thought Dora. —What exactly did her son do, Takis broke in. —Their son had left, the innkeeper replied. —He had gone to the city to live his own life, the old lady added smiling politely.

"That's what he says anyway, he wants to live his own life," the innkeeper continued the conversation, deeply embittered by his son's conduct.

"To our heath!" the others repeated, raising their glasses. Just when a little joy was about to descend upon the table with the final tang of that mythical wine, the old lady again ruined the atmosphere with her sweet, velvet voice. —By the way, where had they put that blackbird?

"We locked it in the bathroom!" Dora replied with apparent cruelty.

WHEN THEY FOUND THEMSELVES BACK IN THEIR ROOM, just before midnight, Dora and Takis were in a state of intense agitation. The moment had finally come for them to spend their first night together. "Did you notice how polite they were?" said Takis as he started to undress. — Dora had been repelled, what exactly had they eaten? Crazy thoughts were going through her mind. — Didn't she like the food? — Oh she had liked the food all right, but would he please tell her what exactly it was that they had eaten? Takis had taken off his trousers. — The fact was that he didn't know for sure what they had eaten. — Dora was nearly going out of her mind, did her companion have the slightest inkling of what she was thinking? — She had ended up making his head reel; whether intentionally or not she had infected him with her anxiety. — Did he remember the moment when that dreadful woman had asked about their bird? — Yes, of course he remembered! — Did he remember their telling her that they had locked it in the bathroom? — Of course, he remembered very well. — Did he remember that after they answered her the woman got up and left the room, supposedly to fetch some fruit? — Yes, he also remembered that, but what was she driving at? He was unable to follow her reasoning.

"Do you think she might have come to our room and killed it?" said Dora, clad only in a provocative

28

slip. Takis froze upon hearing the question. —If they opened the bathroom door, they would know right away if their suspicions were founded. Dora approached the door and with an abrupt movement flung it wide open. The blackbird, startled by the slamming of the door, began to screech nightmarishly:

"Help! I want to live! Help!" Fortunately it had not been harmed. All these hours Takis had been racking his brain to figure out who exactly it was that the blackbird had heard calling for help. Was it a man? Was it a woman? Was he young, old? What was it? —Dora immediately read his thoughts; he suspected that the two old people may have murdered their son. —That's precisely what he was thinking! —Yet Dora's imagination was racing still faster, she suspected that today they may even have eaten a small piece of their son. Takis told her to be quiet; he didn't like to hear such things; they disgusted him.

Dora decided to take a bath before they went to bed. Takis asked her if she had turned on the electric heater. —Yes, she had turned it on before they went down to dinner, his companion replied and went into the bathroom. Just as she was about to turn on the faucet, Takis rushed into the bathroom and stopped her. Dora looked at him in alarm. — Why was he preventing her from taking her bath? Takis said very solemnly that he wanted to check the electric heater. Dora wrapped herself in a blanket and stepped out of the tub. Takis took a wooden stool, climbed on top of it, drew near the electric heater which was located close to the ceiling and carefully began to examine the cables around it. —It was obvious that the cables had been tampered with, someone had done something to the electric heater. If she had taken a bath, she definitely would have been electrocuted. —If they had taken a bath together, both of them would now be dead, Dora thought with horror. —Fortunately he had been guided by God at the last minute and his suspicions had been aroused.

"And would it have looked like an accident?" Dora asked with her heart in her mouth.

"Precisely!" her companion replied and jumped down from the stool. Dora felt dizzy and had to lean somewhere in order not to fall down. Takis took her tenderly by the shoulders and led her to the bed. Her forehead was swimming in perspiration. —Was she feeling better now? he asked. —Yes, now that she was sitting down she felt much better.

"In the end, you were right!" Takis said. "This house is full of deathtraps!" And he reached out with his hand to turn on the lamp that was on the night table and almost next to his pillow. But Dora jumped up and seized his hand. Takis failed to understand her action. —Before turning on the lamp, he should first inspect the switch. After what had happened Dora had started to be suspicious of everything around her. Takis drew near to the switch and began to examine it very carefully. — In fact, it had been dismantled, the first one to make the mistake of turning on the lamp would have been turned to cinders on the spot. — Dora had not expected the two old people to declare themselves so soon. Takis had really begun to be afraid. — How could they go to sleep surrounded by those two old crazies? Dora, however, revealed that she was more coolheaded. — They would lock the door and go to sleep no matter what.

AT LAST DORA AND TAKIS WERE HALF NAKED beneath the bedcovers. The weather conditions were ideal for such games. Outside it was frightfully cold as it normally was in the mountains even at the beginning of spring. The room was snug and warm, the blankets and sheets were spotlessly clean and freshly laundered. Takis was so aroused that he had forgotten how he and his wife, through sheer luck, had narrowly escaped just a little while ago. He was attempting, therefore, to subjugate Dora who was resisting and reacting with grace and various lame arguments to his sexual assaults. — Would he please stop fidgeting? Couldn't he see that she was upset? —All right, but why had they gotten married and come all the way up here, to twiddle their thumbs? —Why was he behaving so shamelessly, wasn't he aware of the situation? — The longer they stayed awake, the better, Takis asserted frenziedly while kissing her frantically on the neck. —This was hardly the way for them to stay awake, couldn't he think of a better way? Dora stammered, attempting to check his momentum. Takis, however, who was exploring her neck with his tongue, was not long in reaching her firm breasts. —Why, he had found the best way possible for them to stay awake, he sputtered half ecstatically from between her breasts, which had begun to quiver and palpitate from inner vibrations despite Dora's will. To bridle the impetuous Takis once and for all, Dora grabbed him by the ears and thrust back his head on top of the pillow. —Quite frankly she marveled at his appetite, his mind was only on one thing. Here the world was coming to an end and he was playing away on his fiddle. —She was clearly driving him mad, but he contained himself and asked with a certain grievance in his voice if in fact they were going to do anything at all! — He would have to be patient and stop being insufferable every five minutes. In the morning, when she was calmer, she might be in the mood to make love.

Takis felt his head reeling; she had unleashed

forces inside him which definitely had to find an outlet, to be blasted into the air. And, as was only natural, he couldn't understand why she was being such a spoilsport again. — The plain truth was that her husband didn't care how others felt, he thought only of himself. — Now what had he done? Takis asked himself foaming at the mouth. He had requested of her the most natural thing in the world. — He knew very well, it was going to be the first time. — So? It had to happen sometime didn't it? — Shouldn't she enjoy it too? Was this any kind of situation for doing that? If he continued to pressure her, there was danger of his traumatizing her psychologically for the rest of her life. — Takis couldn't understand why, if they did it now, this very instant, she wouldn't get as much pleasure out of it as he would? — Couldn't he see that they were in a state of panic? Couldn't he understand her? What if the two old people were observing them through a secret opening in the wall?

That did it. She had gotten the better of him. Takis' sexual desires evaporated into thin air. — Naturally they were observing them, here they were about to murder them, had he forgotten! — In one way or another she had put ideas in his head. — At last he had begun to give some thought to the danger they were in. — In other words, they weren't going to sleep a wink all night? — They would be wise to stay awake and wait for the murderers' next move. — But that would be hell, Takis protested. — Of course it would be hell, but if they wanted to save their lives . . . — Why was she in such a fury, why wouldn't she let them pack their bags and clear out while there was still time? — If she didn't solve this mystery, she felt that she would never regain her calm for as long as she lived. — Very well then, did she have any ideas or were they going to remain like that all night long? — She did have one idea. — Then why hadn't she come out with it? What was she waiting for? — Because he wouldn't let her get in a word edgewise! Well then, they would take the mattresses from the beds and place them on the floor in front of the door. — Takis could not see the purpose of going through all that. — If the two old people had a pass key and tried to enter the room, they would step on them and wake them up, they wouldn't catch them asleep. — He agreed with her, but she would have to get up so that they could transport the mattresses. As they were dragging the mattresses along the floor, Dora suddenly remembered that they had not heard the blackbird for some time. As soon as Takis put down the mattress, he opened the bathroom door and looked inside to see what it was doing. The damned bird was perched on the electric heater sound asleep. As soon as Takis entered the bathroom, however, the blackbird, disturbed by the intrusion, cawed sleepily, "Help!" Takis, exasperated, closed the door behind him so as not to hear it.

THE NEXT MORNING FOUND THEM CHASTE and sleeping soundly on the two mattresses they had dragged from their beds and placed on the floor in front of the door. They must have stayed awake until late into the night, because the day had already advanced considerably and they gave no indication of waking up. Outside the night mist had melted away and a radiant sun and deep blue sky were ushering in one of those early spring days with raw cold and blinding light.

Suddenly they woke with a start terrified. The blackbird, clutching one of the wooden rails of the bed, began to screech hysterically, "Help! Help! He's strangling me! I don't want to die! Help!" Takis had already leaped out of bed and was trying to understand exactly where he was. Dora, his wife, had sat up on the mattress and was rubbing her eyes. — What in the world was going on, she had had a nightmare with a blackbird in it. Takis, who had gone over to the window and opened it, told her to stop shilly-shallying and wake up. Outside it was broad daylight. Dora saw the blackbird on the rails of the bed and pointed at it with horror. — Now what? — It was the bird they had found on the road, didn't she remember it? — Of course she

35

remembered it, she wasn't stupid, that's not what she meant. She distinctly remembered that yesterday they had locked the bird in the bathroom, she also distinctly remembered that the last time he had slammed the door. So how could it be in their room since the bathroom door was still locked? — Takis was agape, how had his wife managed to think of all that when she had just woken up? Deep down she must have been terribly frightened even though she didn't show it.

"Do you think there's a secret entrance?" Dora asked as she got up from the mattress and wrapped a white sheet around her naked body. — Rather, Takis agreed astounded. Dora bent down and examined the lock on the door. It appeared to be intact so they couldn't have come through the door. Takis again went over to the window. This time he stuck his head out and started looking down and around very carefully. The side of the house where their room was situated had been built at the very edge of a frightening vertical cliff whose roots disappeared deep down in a dark ravine. So they couldn't have come through the window either, unless of course they had wings.

Dora recalled again the two incidents with the electric heater and the damaged switch and reminded Takis that they must be extremely careful in their every step and movement. Her husband, however, who was not fully awake yet, was not sure of what his wife had said and started to go into the bathroom to do his morning ablutions. But before he was able to open the door, Dora went and stood in front of him, barring his way. — He couldn't just walk in, she was certain that there was some deathtrap waiting for them in there. Takis, now wide awake, told her that she was absolutely right. He therefore took hold of the doorknob with care, turned it slowly, opened the door and went into the bathroom with countless precautions. Dora, her heart in her mouth, followed behind him. Nothing inside the bathroom seemed to have been altered. The razor blades were exactly as he had left them, the soap was also intact. Dora told him to examine the bottle of cologne. Takis picked it up, removed the stopper with care and brought the mouth of the bottle to his nose. "That's odd, it doesn't smell at all like cologne. I wonder what's inside?" he thought and turned the bottle over in the palm of his hand to see what had happened to the cologne that looked as though it had leaked out. Dora rushed forward and snatched the bottle from him before he could empty any of its contents onto his palm. — For God's sake, why wasn't he more careful? Dora cried out angrily. Afterwards, holding the bottle with horror and walking slowly she proceeded to the washbasin where she poured it down the drain. The washbasin became filled with foam and the water that was standing there started boiling and bubbling loudly. "Why is it doing that?" asked Takis, who was leaning over the washbasin and observing the water. — They had poured out the cologne and put vitriol in the bottle, Dora informed him ready to scream. Takis blanched, turned his face away from the drain and sat down terrified on the edge of the bathtub. — In other words, if he had put on some cologne, he would have been blinded? — Not only blinded but his entire face would have been disfigured, he would have become a monster! Dora consoled him. — How had they gotten in? Takis was racking his brains but couldn't come up with an answer. Dora was asking herself the same question.

From the bedroom the blackbird again began to screech, "Help! Help! He's strangling me! I want to live! I want to live!"

Takis had become dizzy and had begun to see stars, his head felt like it was going to burst. — He would do well to remain seated until he had pulled himself together, Dora advised him. — Now what were they supposed to do? How were they supposed to continue their day? Takis asked himself seated on the edge of the bathtub. They would continue their honeymoon as if nothing had happened. — They would simply get dressed and go downstairs to breakfast, Dora said to him, certain that Takis would be of the same mind. — He agreed in principle, Takis replied and stood up. His mind, however, was now spinning at the rate of a thousand revolutions a minute. He wanted to tell her something but did not know what, he wanted her to be careful, now that she was about to get dressed she should be very careful and not put on any of her jewelry.

"Why?" his companion asked surprised. — She knew what he meant, there was little point in explaining it to her. — She had no idea what he meant; besides she hadn't brought anything with her except a diamond pin given to her by her mother. — It was the very thing that she mustn't put on, Takis insisted. Dora was still without a clue. — The idea had crossed his mind that they may have put poison on the needle of the pin. "That's impossible!" Dora stammered, panic-stricken, and she became angry with herself for not having thought of it first before her husband had told her. — All she had to do was scratch her hand with the needle while putting on the pin and that would be it, the show would be over, good-bye folks. Dora came out of the bathroom in a frenzy and went straight to the suitcase that concealed the diamond pin. She wanted to find out if Takis' suspicions were at all founded. Her companion dashed some water on his face and went into the bedroom. — Well? Had she found the pin? Dora was standing in the middle of the room white as a sheet, holding the diamond pin in her palms. She was trembling all over and about to faint. — What happened, why was she acting this way? — The pocket of the suitcase that concealed the pin was open!

"Was the case with the pin also open?" Takis asked out of curiosity. — Yes, it had also been opened and then discarded at the bottom of the suitcase. If he wanted to, he could come closer and see for himself, at the tip of the needle there was something liquidlike that was shining. She brought it near his face so that he could see better. Takis leaped back. — What did she think she was doing! She should be careful with that poison, it's probably very dangerous. — The murderer didn't have time to zip the pocket shut, nor did he have time to put the pin back in its case. It seemed that at the crucial moment the blackbird must have called out and, afraid that they would wake up, he had hurriedly tossed the pin into the pocket of the suitcase and fled. — But what if it had all been planned that way so that, without suspecting, she would put her hand in the pocket of the suitcase and prick herself? Takis asked without giving it much thought, thus adding to Dora's fright. — There was no doubt about it, Dora thought, it had all been planned that way so that she would prick herself without realizing it. From now on they would have to watch their every step. Those two old people were extremely dangerous.

WHEN THEY WENT DOWNSTAIRS to the dining room to breakfast, it was nearly noon. The spring sun had made the large room so warm that the two innkeepers had thrown open the two large glass doors situated on the eastern side of the hall. These doors led to the exterior, to an immense veranda full of flower beds with flowers in full bloom and which, inflamed by the bright light, gave off a sweet smell. It was almost hot. This was why the old couple had dragged the table where the two newlyweds were to have their breakfast next to an open glass door. They had positioned the chairs in such a way that the sun reached as far as the legs of the two newlyweds in order to keep them both warm, while the rest of their body remained in the hospitable shade of the dining room in order somehow to remain cool. The breakfast that the old lady had prepared for them was sumptuous, worthy of warriors who have been away in battle for months, far from their homes and who one fine morning, quite unexpectedly, return to their native soil, total physical wrecks. When they saw them descending the stairs in good spirits and well-dressed, the two old people bid them good morning with delight. The young couple returned their greetings with a smile. —Well, how had things gone, did they get a

41

good night's sleep? the innkeeper's wife asked as she placed a crystal jar with yellow marmalade on the table. — As far as sleep went, no way, Dora said mincing her words. The innkeeper, however, misunderstood her, thinking they had stayed awake for the obvious reasons that newlyweds stay awake, and in spite of himself he clapped his hands feebly three times while shouting, "Bravo! Bravo!"

The table which with its multicolored cheer was glowing and smelled delicious had, without their realizing it, gathered all of them around it. — Goodness what was all this that they had prepared for them, Takis said in admiration looking at the table. — They couldn't possibly eat all that, Dora, carried away by the exotic abundance of the morning spread, marveled with pleasure. "You must eat well, especially at a time like this!" the old lady said with a sly smile as she placed a puffed up cake in the center of the table. — His wife had remembered the good old times and done her utmost to please them, the old innkeeper told them. "Come, let's sit down!" the old lady suggested sweetly and was the first to pull out a chair and be seated. Without saying another word the others eagerly followed her example. Soon they were all seated around the cheerful morning table. — What smelled so good? asked Takis trying with his nose to locate the delectable source of this aroma which was enough to make you faint. — It was probably the hotcakes, she had also made hotcakes for them, the old lady said. — But why were they sitting there looking at them? Why didn't they start? What were they waiting for, the old man asked himself. Why, of course, he had forgotten, his wife had to say her customary prayer. Bravo kids for having thought of it! He was very favorably impressed. The old lady crossed her hands on the table and began to pray with a stone-like, immobile, nearly dead face — a serene face which had grown accustomed to the idea of death and in whose small, gray wrinkles nothing was able to awaken emotion any more. "We thank you, O Lord, for allowing us to reach dawn and to enjoy one more day, safe and sound, with our table filled with your riches. Forgive us and make us deserving of such happiness always, amen!" The morning prayer of the old lady had for some strange reason made them gloomy. No one felt like eating. — Why didn't they start, what were they waiting for? the old man asked the young couple. — They were waiting for the food to cool off, Dora replied. Takis was of the same mind, that's why he was waiting too. "Ah, but if the food gets cold, it won't taste good!" the old lady said and began filling her dish with various tasty morsels. — They should eat it now while it was still warm, if it gets cold it won't be any good, the innkeeper, who had already filled his plate to the top and begun to nibble, also exhorted them.

Dora was terror stricken and did not know where to begin. She was watching to see what the old lady put on her plate and to emulate her. So as not to appear to be scrutinizing everything, every so often, whenever she wanted to taste something, she would first offer it to Takis. He had attacked the food without the slightest reservation and in order to reciprocate the savory attentions of his wife he would, from time to time and without being conscious of what he was doing, also offer her small bites that the suspicious Dora was obliged to swallow without, of course, being able to ascertain each time whether or not they were poisoned. Delicious, she would say, very tasty, she would remark. But her terror was such that she could no longer distinguish among the different tastes and would repeatedly ask the old lady, supposedly out of politeness, to tell them what exactly it was that they were eating. But she — the old meanie — refused to reveal her secret recipes. Dora sensed that she would soon faint if this agony continued much longer. In fact, she had turned pale and her forehead was covered with cold perspiration. The innkeeper, who was observing her out of the corner of his eye, realized that something terrible was happening to her. Dora slowly leaned forward and rested her head on the table. Takis jumped up and started shouting: "Give her some water! For God's sake, give her some water!" The innkeeper's wife filled a glass with cold water and handed it to him. Takis sat Dora up, leaned her head against the back of the chair and brought the glass to her lips. Dora drank one or two gulps of the cold water and began to recover her senses.

"Thank you!" she stammered and tried to sit up in her chair as if nothing had happened.

"Do you feel better?" Takis asked with concern. —Yes, she felt much better now. They mustn't worry, the crisis was over, they could continue with their meal peacefully. —What had happened? Takis asked, seated at his place with a cup full of steaming hot coffee in his hand. —For a moment she had felt giddy, but now she was fine.

—There was only one thing in this whole business that the old innkeeper couldn't understand. — Takis looked at him with alarm, what business was he referring to and what exactly was it that he couldn't understand? —The old innkeeper asked him straight out how it came about that he had remembered them after so many years. The old lady saw the surprise in the young man's eyes and attempted to justify her husband's question. —The only reason he was asking was that all the others had forgotten them, even thinking they had died many years ago. —We sometimes think the same, the innkeeper added, smiling bitterly. Dora did not catch his humor and to be sure that she had heard correctly she asked him again, "What do you think?" —That we've already died, the old lady replied immediately breaking out into a harsh, full laugh. They all felt so strange that in order to overcome the unbearable situation that had been created they broke out into a mirthful, nervous and unbridled laugh. When they had descended all the steps of their jolly hysteria and had finally arrived at the bottom on some landing of silence and composure, Takis decided that the time had come to take the reins of speech in his hands and to speak in his defense. — How did he happen to remember them after so many years? Why he had liked their place a lot. They used to enjoy themselves so much then, in the old days. All the guests at the small inn were like one big happy family. There was a great deal of joy at that time in their small inn. His wife's cooking. The warm, lovely hospitality of the innkeeper. They all felt like one family. He wanted his wife Dora to experience that same happiness. He wanted to make her understand the kind of household he was expecting from her. The sort of atmosphere he'd like their home to have now that they were finally married. He stopped talking but his words continued to echo in their hearts. "He wanted to train me, that's why he brought me to this wilderness!" Dora added as an epilogue to Takis' short, moving speech. — They must forgive them, they weren't to blame if with time their inn had deteriorated and no one ever set foot there. With time, as the years went by, they had fallen

46

into a "rut" and their soul had dried up. Then gradually everyone had left. Thus their little hotel had become empty. — But what exactly had happened? Dora asked, full of curiosity. — Why had this happened to them? Takis followed close behind with his question.

"We saw!" the innkeeper answered monosyllabically.

"What in God's name did you see?" Dora intervened, dreadfully uneasy.

"We saw what you cannot yet see!" the old lady answered enigmatically.

"But what was it that you saw?" Takis insisted.

"It is unspeakable!" she replied. "When you say it, you bring evil upon yourself!"

"You shrivel up when you come to know what it is!" the innkeeper added. — Since one way or another they would find out what it was, why didn't they tell them now so that they could get it over with once and for all, Dora suggested. — They were still too young to learn what it is. When they grew old, they would find out for themselves.

"Do you think we'll ever grow old?" Dora reflected.

"That's what we all used to say when we were young!" the innkeeper informed her.

"That's what we all used to say. 'Do you think we'll ever grow old?'" the old lady repeated and her eyes filled with tears.

IT WAS A GORGEOUS DAY SO DORA AND TAKIS DECIDED to get into their car and drive to the top of the mountain to see the old fortress. They had barely finished their breakfast before they had already gotten into their car and fled, as if pursued, far from that bizarre old couple. Now they were in their car and amidst the thousand bends in the road they were heading straight for the top of the mountain. — They were quite right to get away from them for a little while. Takis indeed felt relieved of a great weight. — They really had been in danger during breakfast. One of the dishes must have been poisoned, said Dora who still hadn't recovered from that ordeal with the food. — They weren't out of danger yet, Takis added. The fact that they were far away from them didn't mean a thing, the poison contained in the food could take effect twelve hours later. "Do you think we should notify the police?" Dora asked, looking at him with frightened eyes. Takis, however, appeared self-composed and was driving in high spirits. — No, he replied, it was too soon for that. — The thought of returning to that depressing inn made her heart sink. — He had told her from the start that they should pack their bags and clear out, but she had insisted on solving the mystery first. — He was absolutely right, she was the one who had insisted. —Maybe she felt they should go straight back, pack their bags and leave right this minute without another thought? —No, she felt they should remain, she wanted to find out what exactly was going on in that mysterious inn. —In that case she mustn't complain. —If they managed to survive, she was certain that they would discover something terrible which might even change their lives. —Did she really think that they would discover something terrible? Takis asked mechanically as he drove round the bends of the narrow road like a madman. — Of course, Dora assured him, her instinct was never wrong. —But they would be better off forgetting all that for a little while and enjoying the view, Takis suggested. — Dora was of the same opinion, they would be better off forgetting all that for a little while.

—By the way, did she know where they were going? her husband asked. —To visit some ancient ruins, she replied looking out the window. —Not exactly ancient ruins, they were going to visit an old fortress at the top of the mountain. —The view from up there was spectacular, Dora observed. —It certainly was, everything was visible, even the sea and various islands. —Nice weather, Dora murmured. —Very nice, Takis agreed. A great massacre had taken place there in the past. —Things like that were always happening in the past, Dora mumbled with an air of clear disapproval. —Of course, Takis continued, the various wars prevented people from growing old.

"They were horrible times!" Dora concluded. — Of course they were horrible times, Takis agreed. Just as people were about to put their lives in some kind of order and settle down, war would break out and it was back to square one again. — How many more bends before they reached the top? asked Dora who already was beginning to feel dizzy. — They were going to drive through ravines of such extraordinary beauty that she wouldn't believe her eyes. "Ravines?" asked Dora full of misgivings. — Yes, ravines, chasms and valleys suspended between heaven and earth. "Stop the car!" Dora screamed.

Takis was taken aback, now what was wrong? — She wanted to get out! — What was the matter, why did she want to get out? — They had to get out, she would explain what the matter was after they got out. Takis was forced to pull up alongside the road on a curve. Dora opened the door and jumped out terrified. Takis followed after her. — What was wrong? Did she feel dizzy? — Had he checked the car at all before they left? Dora asked pale as a sheet. — No, he hadn't! — Then he should do it right now! — What in blazes was he supposed to check? her husband asked annoyed. — He should check the brakes!

"Do you think?" stammered Takis, whose suspicions were now aroused and who had finally begun to catch on. —Yes, she was certain that they had done something to the brakes. Takis removed his jacket and crawled under the car.

"Find anything?" asked Dora, who was standing over him. —Not yet, the car brakes were in order, they hadn't been touched. Instead of coming out from under the car, however, Takis crawled almost completely under it. There was one more thing he wanted to check.

"This is horrible, Dora, simply horrible!" he could be heard saying from under the car. —What had he found that was horrible, had they planted a bomb? —No, something worse, Takis informed her, coming out from under the car and shaking the dust from his clothes. The tie rod had been filed. —The "tie rod"? She was hearing the word for the first time. What was that? —A piece of steel that connected the steering wheel and the wheels. —What would happen if it broke? —If it broke, they would lose control of the car. —Was he saying that this tie rod could break on one of the curves? —Right, and they'd fall into a ravine! —They were ultimately determined to do them in at any cost! —Right again, Takis said, and asked her what she thought they should do now. —Could they drive back to the inn without any risk of ending up in some ravine? —Sure, if they drove slowly they wouldn't be in much danger, her husband replied.

— In that case, it was back to the inn, Dora said stubbornly and got into the car.

TAKIS STOPPED THE CAR at a considerable distance from the inn. Dora couldn't understand why he had pulled up at that spot. — They would get out of the car and go the rest of the way on foot so as not to attract the attention of the two old people. — Why should they go through all that? Dora asked. — They would creep up on them and listen at the kitchen window which was still open in order to hear what they were saying. Dora had to admit that she never would have thought of anything like that and followed her husband, who had taken a narrow footpath in the woods as a short-cut.

IT WAS NOT YET AFTERNOON AND THE SUN'S LIGHT was still vertical and harsh. The heat during the past two or three hours, as long as midday lasted, had remained steadfast. Everything had heated up as if it were already summer. The two old people were in the kitchen of the small inn. The woman was ironing on a large wooden table and the innkeeper, seated in an old leather armchair, was cleaning his carbine with great care. They had left the kitchen window wide open to somehow stay cool. It was the first time all spring that it was so hot, yet the forest, earth and rocks, regardless of how heated they had become, retained something of the winter humidity. This is why the breeze that was wafted into the house was pleasant and refreshing. The young couple, taking a thousand and one precautions, had approached the kitchen window. The two old people were talking about something.

"Poor kids!" the old lady said sadly while ironing a white sheet. — Why "poor kids"? asked her husband as he cleaned the barrel of his carbine. — Didn't he know why? his wife said ironically without looking up from the sheet she was ironing. — In the end they had demoralized those two young people, her husband observed.

"Do you think they suspect what's in store for them?" the old woman asked as naturally as possible while placing the hot iron on its metal stand. — Of course they suspected, they weren't fools. Didn't she notice the way they were looking at them?

"Things don't always turn out the way one expects!" the woman said and sighed. — The old man proposed to go to their room and open the window so that that damned bird would fly away. — Why was he irritated by the bird? — How could he not be irritated by it? It was always coming out with the truth!

Dora and Takis raised their heads and looked

through the kitchen window to see what the two old people were doing, because all of a sudden they had stopped talking. The woman was ironing and the old man was cleaning his carbine. "Did he call?" the woman asked the old innkeeper quite unexpectedly.

"Did who call?" the old man asked absentmindedly. — He knew very well who called them, so why ask? The old man discerned who she meant right away. — What did he want calling? It would be better if he left them alone. — He had told her that he would come at midnight to have a word with them. — Did she inform him that there were people at the inn? — Yes, that's why he told her that he would come at midnight. After this exchange the two old people fell silent again. Dora and Takis, who had grown tired from stooping, had each taken up a position at one of the corners of the window, and half hidden in this way they went on listening carefully to all that the two old people were saying.

The first to start speaking was the innkeeper. — He asked his wife if these two would make it! At first she didn't know who he was talking about. — About the newlyweds, who else? "Depends!" the woman replied monosyllabically.

"Depends on what?" the old man asked bluntly. — If they really loved each other, there was some hope of their being saved, his wife informed him with a deep sigh. — The old innkeeper was of the

54

same opinion, if they really loved each other, there was great hope of their being saved.

WHEN TAKIS AND DORA FOUND THEMSELVES back in their room, they were frantic. They had been thrown into a tailspin by what they had heard. "Did you hear them?" Dora kept saying as she walked back and forth in the room in a state of turmoil. — How could he not have heard them? — When all was said and done those two old people were guilty! Dora exclaimed fuming with rage. — There was no doubt about that, her companion assured her. — But who could they have killed? — Probably their son, Takis concluded. — That was hard to believe. Did he think they actually killed their own son? she repeated mechanically looking at Takis strangely.

"Most likely!" Takis said and even conjectured that the blackbird may have belonged to their son. — But what could have made them kill their own son? — Maybe he went astray, Takis, who always had an answer for everything, replied. — Was that a reason for killing their own child? — Who could know what was going on in their heads, two old people like that who were half-crazy from living in solitude. — They really were a bizarre couple, Dora murmured to herself and fell silent because her mind had stopped functioning.

Takis, however, was not about to let up. —Who did she think called them? Upon hearing Takis' latest question Dora was immediately brought back to reality. —Did he mean the person coming at midnight? "That's precisely who I mean!" Takis muttered. Dora was unable to conjecture anything at all about the person who was to visit the two old people at midnight. —The best thing for them to do was to wait and see who it was with their own eyes. —As far as Takis was concerned, he was convinced that the person coming at midnight was a key player in this affair.

All these conjectures and suppositions had ended by making Dora dizzy. She wanted them to stop for a while so that she could put some order in her thoughts. But her husband wouldn't leave her alone. —Had she heard the other thing? "What other thing?" Dora asked frightened.

"That there were other people at the hotel!" Takis replied. —He shouldn't be silly, there weren't any other people at the hotel, the innkeepers had been alluding to the two of them. —It wasn't all that simple, Takis continued. He was almost certain that something terrible was going on inside that godforsaken inn, he was convinced that those two old people were doing something terrible with their victims. Dora felt as if she was choking, she was unable to breathe normally, she was having difficulty. —What did he think of what they had said about the two of them? — What could he think? It had given him the shivers! — And why, might she ask, had it given him the shivers? — Didn't she realize that those two old people had taken it into their head to kill them? Takis replied irritably. If they didn't really love one another, if they didn't really care about one another, they would already have been dead by now. This thought made her burst into heartrending tears. Takis approached her and tried to console her. — What was the matter? Until a little while ago she was the one who was brave. What had happened all of a sudden to make her lose her nerve? — She was crying because they had been together for two nights and with all that was happening they had not found a moment's peace to enjoy their love, they were at the breaking point. — She mustn't worry, Takis said putting his arms around her and kissing her hair tenderly. When this was all over, they would have their entire lives before them to enjoy their love. Dora managed somehow to calm down; she had the impression that this entire matter had brought them closer together. Takis thought so too; all these ordeals had bonded them more.

The blackbird, clutching a corner of the large walnut wardrobe, began to screech luridly, "Help! Help! He's strangling me! Help! I want to live! I want to live! I don't want to die! Help! Help!" By now, however, Dora and Takis were used to it and paid no attention. Suddenly Takis rushed to the window and drew the curtains, he had heard an automobile pulling up to the inn. — What time was it by the way? Dora looked at her watch. — It was twelve o'clock! — Perfect, said Takis, it must be the mysterious stranger. He had finally come! He was very punctual. — Were they going to go downstairs and eavesdrop? Dora asked timidly. — They were going to go downstairs and eavesdrop, but they would have to be very careful, they mustn't make the slightest noise.

THE YOUNG COUPLE HAD CONCEALED themselves upstairs, behind the thick wooden balusters of the staircase which led down to the living room, and were following with bated breath the proceedings in the semi-obscurity downstairs.

The two old people had turned off all the lights so that the space was illuminated only by the flames from the chimney. A young man with the face of a child and light brown hair had his back turned to them and was looking at the fire in silence. The old innkeeper was sitting in his customary old chair. His wife was standing behind him, her hands resting lightly on the back of the seat.

The woman was the first to speak; she asked the

58

young man to tell her why he had suddenly remembered them. Without turning to look at them, he
replied that he always remembered them. — Of
course he remembered them. Whenever he needed
money, he remembered them before anyone else,
the innkeeper said. The young man turned and
stared at him. The innkeeper's wife, in a voice shat-
tered by emotion, asked the young man what he
was doing. How was he was getting along?

"Splendidly!" he replied sharply, and looked
around for something to drink. The innkeeper,
however, was unyielding with the young man. — He
would very much like to know who was paying for
his "splendid" life. "Various people," the young
man replied with cynicism. — Was he trying to tell
them that he had also become a thief? his mother
asked, ready to burst into tears. — If only that was
all he had become, the young man replied as he
filled a glass with cognac from a bottle that happened to be lying around. The wife of the innkeeper
had begun to weep silently.

"Why is our child so desperate?" she ventured
stammering. — They were the ones, his own parents, who had driven him to despair, the young
man threw in her face with contempt. — How were
they to blame, they had only done what was best!
murmured the old lady looking at the fire with
tearful eyes. The young man's face had turned dark
red; with one abrupt movement he emptied the

contents of the glass into the flames. The fire flared up momentarily.

"My soul became cramped living in here all those years!" he screamed at his parents. — But how had they harmed him? his mother asked, ready to unleash her tears. — They had practically killed him by their behavior, the young man shouted, kicking a small stool with his foot. The innkeeper, however, was unperturbed by his son's anger. — What did he want from them? he asked him slowly. Hadn't they always given him what he asked for?

The young man started shouting and walking around them like a maniac, his face dripping with perspiration from rage and anger. — They were always measuring and weighing things. For as long as he could remember they were always measuring and weighing things. In the meantime life was passing by, running out, yet there they were, entering their gains and losses in their grimy ledger. Even in their sleep they were measuring and weighing things. They never stopped counting, two small ants counting and gnawing life. The innkeeper, without getting up from his seat, told him very simply that they were not rich and he would do well not to forget that when he took it into his head to insult them. Life had forced them to live the way they did, his mother apprised him, wiping away her tears with a handkerchief. But by now the young man was good and angry. — They had even counted him, they had even entered him in their grimy ledger. He was standing in front of them, shouting as if he wanted to kill them with his cries. — He too was nothing but a small piece in their lousy schemes. His mother, unable to endure any more, buried her face in her hands. — So their son loathed them that much? They had only his best interests at heart, they had not wanted him to end up the way he did, his father said sadly. — And just how had they wanted him to end up, like them? the young man asked, scoffing at them one more time.

"At least we love each other!" his mother ventured to say, entangling her words from emotion. — At least they had accomplished that, the father continued bitterly. — Whereas he would live to regret what he was doing, his mother stammered sobbing. — And supposing he didn't live to regret it, then what? their son said, bursting into tears and laughter. — In any event, they had always thought of his well-being, the innkeeper said in his distress, but he had taken it the wrong way. One day he would understand them, but by then it would be too late. They weren't heroes, they were ordinary people. Ordinary people who would never forget that he was their son. If anything should ever happen to him, they would always help him as long as they were alive. If anything should ever happen to him, his parents would always be there, up there in their small inn waiting for him. If he was ever in danger, he must never hesitate, he must come running at once and knock on their door. They had no one else in the world. While he was away, they had managed to save a little money.

"Here, take it, you can have it!" the old innkeeper said abandoning his chair for the first time and placing a bundle of paper bills on a table. — The money was his, only they wanted him to understand them. They had done their best for him in life. They wanted him to understand them and not hate them. Life had forced them to live the way they had lived. Life . . . They had never intended to hurt him. They only wanted to protect him, to make him strong. But they hadn't done a very good job of it! Oh well . . . Things don't always happen the way we want. The son, who all this time had remained motionless with his head down, approached the table, grabbed the money, stuffed it in one of his pockets and nearly ran out of the house. He did not want his parents to see him crying from emotion.

DORA AND TAKIS RETURNED TO THEIR ROOM on tiptoe. Once they were inside the room and had closed the door behind them, they heaved a deep sigh of relief. The frightening scene they had observed a few moments ago had, for some inexplicable reason, filled them with anguish. The first thing Dora thought of after regaining her composure somewhat was where the two old people had found the money that they gave their son. Takis, in good faith, reckoned that they had probably put something aside from their pension. —What stuff and nonsense was he talking about, pension rubbish! — She obviously had another explanation, but would she mind being a little more specific?

"I think I've solved the mystery!" Dora murmured, her eyes flashing. —Would she please hurry up and tell him what she suspected? "They kill and rob whoever happens to come up here and give the money to that preposterous son of theirs," Dora replied. —Why was he standing there with his mouth open and not saying a word? —Now that she had said it, she did seem right. —There it was in a nutshell, Dora concluded almost with relief.

Takis, however, did not think it was all that simple. They had to have an accomplice in their crimes. —What did they need with an accomplice? Dora asked quizzically. —They were too old to manage by themselves, they needed someone younger for the heavy work. —Did he in other words think that the son helped them kill the unsuspecting guests and get rid of the bodies? — Precisely, the son was their accomplice. —And what role did the blackbird play in this grisly tale?

— It must have belonged to one of their victims. The bird witnessed the murder of its master and then, without their realizing it, beat it. — In other words, according to his speculations it was as if he was telling her that tonight the two old people would act more decisively. — That's precisely what he was telling her. Since death by misadventure had not worked, they would take more drastic steps. — Dora agreed with him completely, they would try to murder them tonight at any cost. — In that case the best thing for them to do was to pack their bags and leave while there was still time, Takis suggested. — No, they would stay there and expose them, Dora said with determination. God alone knows how many innocent travelers they had murdered and would go on murdering if they weren't stopped.

— Supposing they had a pistol, how would they defend themselves? her companion asked her and quite rightly. — Dora did not believe that the two old people would use a pistol. — But supposing— even if it was one chance in a million—that they did use one? Takis insisted. — In that case, said Dora, they would also use theirs. — What pistol was she talking about? As far as he knew, they had none. — Oh but they did, Dora replied solemnly, opening her handbag and taking out a small pistol with an ivory handle. Takis took it in his hands. He was flabbergasted. — What in the world was this?

—It was a pistol, couldn't he see?

"It looks like a toy!" Takis muttered. —A toy, but one that did a neat little job! —So she had a pistol and had never mentioned it to him? —She always carried a pistol with her. Takis could not grasp what exactly it was that his dear wife was saying to him. —When she was young, some brute had attacked her, Dora tried to explain. —Next she would be telling him that he had also raped her? Takis interrupted her. —He needn't worry, she had been and still was a virgin; she had managed to get away before the brute could harm her. —Why in all this time had she never told him about her youthful adventures? —They didn't concern him, all that mattered at present was that the brute who attacked her had not succeeded in raping or harming her. —What were they going to do now? Takis asked frightfully worried. —They would lie down and wait for the two old people to make their appearance. —What about the light? —They would turn it off as soon as they got into bed. —Were they going to stay awake all night long in the dark? That would be sheer torture, Takis thought. But Dora who had already lain down, turned off the switch over the bed and the room was plunged into darkness.

TOTAL DARKNESS. SUDDENLY THE SOUND of a light switch is heard— "click"—and the light goes on. It is after midnight. We are upstairs in Takis and Dora's room. Takis is seated on the bed, prodding a hair dryer with a fork. Dora, seated on the other side of the bed, is prodding Takis' electric razor with a bent hairpin. The sudden dispersion of light has startled them. Their faces are harsh, full of hatred and malice. "Who turned on the light?" Takis asks angrily. It certainly wasn't Dora, she wouldn't have wanted him to catch her in the act of tampering with his electric shaver for anything in the world. —So she wasn't asleep yet, Takis said as he approached her threateningly with the dismantled hair dryer in his hands. He didn't frighten Dora though. They were playing tit for tat. —From what she could see, he wasn't asleep either. Afterwards her eye caught sight of his night table. —The glass of milk that she had brought him had not been touched. —Nor had the glass of water that she had asked him to bring her been touched, Takis observed. —What a shame, and she had put a soporific in his milk, he would have fallen asleep and not been aware of anything. —He had also put a soporific in her water. He would not have had the courage to strangle her if she had been awake, she would have raised the roof with her screams. —But what was she doing holding his electric shaver? — She was attempting to dismantle it so that she would have the pleasure of seeing him burnt to cinders when he started to shave. — He was attempting to do the same with her hair dryer.

— So he hated her that much? — She had lied to him, he could never forgive her that. — He had never loved her, all that interested him was to find out if, in fact, he was the first one. — He had made his position clear on that subject from the beginning, he didn't want a used woman! — In the last analysis he was also a rapist in his way. — Perhaps, but he had not tried to trap her, to deceive her, he had been perfectly frank with her from the beginning. — When you came right down to it that mutt she had married could hardly be characterized as a human being, Dora thought. — If they had made love the first night and he had discovered that she had lied to him, he would have let her electrocute herself with the water from the electric heater. Dora, however, had also taken her precautions. — If she had discovered that he intended to abandon her, she would have let him turn on the broken reading lamp so that she might have the pleasure of seeing him burnt to cinders right beside her. — What Takis had difficulty understanding was why she had put vitriol in his bottle of cologne. — For the same reason that he had put poison on her mother's pin. The first night he might not have turned on the reading lamp, just as she might not have taken a bath. In the morning, however, she wanted to punish him at any cost if he intended to abandon her because she was no longer a virgin. She would have blinded him and then he would have been completely at her mercy for the rest of his life. — He had also decided to take her life with her mother's pin.

— He must have realized at noon that she was the one behind all the mystery as a way of forestalling the consummation of their marriage. — Yes, at noon he was nearly certain that she had lied to him. That's why he had taken a file and filed the tie rod, he wanted them to die together. Still he wasn't altogether certain that she had deceived him, that's why he left it to chance. Precisely, he had thought that if she suspected what he had done before it was too late, well then, that would have been the sign that the time for them to die had not yet come. They kept postponing and postponing the time of their death. — Was it possible that they really loved each other? Dora asked smiling diabolically. — They kept postponing it, Takis said to her, because neither he nor she was certain, that is, they had not yet found out what they were trying to find out. — According to his version, in the end it was the blackbird that had saved them. — Yes, without it everything would have been over the first night.

— And what did he intend to do now, Dora asked Takis in a cold tone of voice, ready to attack him.

"I'm going to kill you with my bare hands!" Takis said softly and began to approach her threateningly. — Was he all that certain that she had lied to him? His eyes had become glazed and as he drew nearer to her he kept opening and closing his hands mechanically. — It was possible, of course, that she had been raped and that she wasn't at all to blame.

"It's true!" Dora stammered, drawing back. — One more lie that she had fabricated to confuse him and lead him down the garden path. Dora placed her hand under her pillow and produced the pistol with the small ivory handle. — If he took one more step, she would not hesitate in the least, she would shoot him, after that it didn't matter what happened. Takis, however, was determined to strangle her with his own hands. — If he came any closer, she would pull the trigger. But Takis, as if in a hypnotic trance, was oblivious to her words.

With outstretched hands and firm steps he advanced toward her, uttering through clenched teeth, "Liar, liar!" Dora aimed the pistol at him. — If he took one more step . . . Ultimately she had married a brute, a cold-blooded killer. With one precipitate movement Takis knocked the pistol out of her hands and seized her by the neck. He began to squeeze. Dora screamed and tried to resist. But Takis continued to squeeze, repeating mechanically, "Liar! Liar!"

Dora tried to escape, screaming, "Help! Help! He's strangling me! I want to live! I don't want to die!"

The blackbird, clutching the wardrobe, placidly repeated the same words, "Help! Help! He's strangling me! He's strangling me! I want to live! I want to live! I don't want to die!"

The large walnut wardrobe began to creak and move slowly along the wall toward the corner of the room. In a little while the innkeeper and his wife appeared at the opening of a secret entrance that revealed itself behind the wardrobe. "Would you please calm down!" the old innkeeper and his wife said coldly in unison to the young couple that was still fighting next to the bed. "We're right here and we can see you!"

Dora and Takis, after some time and considerable effort, managed to comprehend what was happening and without further ado decided to pretend that they were reacting to their presence. Their surprise was such, however, that Takis let go of Dora's neck at the very moment when the irreparable was about to happen. —Where in blazes did they come from? Dora asked coughing and holding her bruised neck. —She could see for herself that behind the wardrobe there was a secret entrance, thus her question was quite unnecessary, the old innkeeper replied sternly.

"Were you the ones who turned on the light in

the middle of the night?" Takis asked as he sank down exhausted on the bed. — They were indeed the ones who had turned on the light, the old lady informed him. All these days they had been observing them at close range. "What do you want now?" Takis, who in the meantime had regained some of his strength, asked somewhat aggressively.

"We won't allow this terrible thing to happen, at least not in our house!" the innkeeper's wife said with determination.

"She wants us to base our life on a lie," Takis informed them, pointing at his wife with hatred.

"He's a brute," she replied, "how can I spend an entire lifetime with a brute?" The two old people began to speak. — Neither was his wife lying, nor naturally was her husband a brute! Something else was making them afraid. Something else was nearly driving them mad!

— If they knew what it was, then why didn't they tell them so they would also know!

— The life on which they were about to embark, the old couple continued, was what was making them afraid and nearly driving them mad. They thought the life they were about to start building together would mean the loss of their freedom. It was these two old people who were causing this endless fear in them. Would they end up like them? This is what they kept asking themselves and their minds were slowly becoming muddled from fear.

71

The same thing that was frightening their son frightened them. Only things weren't quite like that, the innkeeper and his venerable wife continued with their little sermon. The two of them really loved each other. This is why at the last minute they told each other their deep, dark secrets and would not allow death to be set free, to come between them and separate them forever.

Dora and Takis listened in silence seated on the edge of their bed and with their heads bowed as the two old people went on with their advice. What they had to understand now was that for a relationship to win out sacrifices were necessary. He had to forget and his wife had to turn a blind eye. The time had come for them to love each other more deeply. The time had come for them to put aside their solitude which they mistook for liberty. The time had come for them to take each other's hand and to march forward together in life. It's a wonderful feeling knowing that you're growing old with a companion next to you. You mellow, you become a man! It's a wonderful feeling sharing your sleep with someone else. They mustn't be afraid. The moment had come for them to join hands and to feel compassion for one another. They mustn't be afraid! They must join hands and truly love one another.

Dora and Takis stood up, approached each other and embraced with expressionless, numb faces.

They were not yet accustomed to the notions of sacrifice and love in their life and felt somewhat awkward. The old lady approached the blackbird and beckoned it to sit on her shoulder. The bird in a single flutter came and perched lightly on her right shoulder. — Her husband had given her this blackbird when they were married. — The two of them, the old innkeeper continued, had also reached the same impasse at the beginning of their marriage. — The words that the blackbird kept repeating were her words, the old lady informed them. It had heard them from her. They had behaved just like them at the beginning of their marriage. — It was true, he had tried to strangle his wife when they were young, the innkeeper murmured. But their love and forgiveness had won out.

"Time for us to set it free!" the woman said and went over to the window.

"It may save others," the innkeeper murmured throwing the window wide open. The sky had begun to grow rosy-hued. The bird spread its black wings in the diaphanous sky and flew far away.

"Join hands! Join hands and love one other! Don't be afraid! Don't be afraid!" the blackbird could be heard shouting from high above as it flew straight into the heart of dawn. The dark ravine below on the earth echoed with the sweet sound of its orders. When the blackbird had disappeared into the morning light, the old lady took Dora by the hand. — Time for them to go down to the kitchen and for her to teach Dora her recipes. They must leave the men by themselves so that they could play their game of chess.

REPLAY

MARCUS HAD BEEN RELEASED FROM PRISON three days ago. He had remained behind bars for fifteen years and was no longer all that young. His aged mother had died from grief and he had no one else in the world. For three days now he had been wandering about in the city like a stray dog. The little money they had given him was nearly gone and he did not know what to do.

He would sleep on some bench and spend the day in a café. He wanted to work, but who would hire him dressed the way he was. And even if someone should turn up who felt sorry for him, he had never learned to do anything. That afternoon he had reached the end of his rope. His money all but gone, he had bought a newspaper for company and had sat down in a café, waiting.

As he was passing a kiosk, his eye had been struck by a multicolored pen — one of those cheap kinds — and he had bought it. He had also bought a block of paper. These two small objects would come to his rescue, he thought, though even he was not sure how. He had left them on the table next to the coffee cup where he would look at them and take courage in their colors. At some point he decided to open the newspaper to the page with the want ads. His eyes became fixed on a strange ad and he took the pen and underlined it.

"Well-to-do middle-aged woman wants to meet young man. Seeks only daily companionship and friendship." He would go find her at once — her house was somewhere downtown — and he would go on foot.

HE FOUND THE HOUSE EASILY but could not bring himself to knock on the door. It was a palace. He circled around the place for hours, observing it without having the courage to knock on the door. He began to feel dizzy and held on to the balustrade so as not to collapse in the street. As soon as it began to grow dark, however, he became alarmed. He too wanted to plant himself somewhere, he no longer had the strength to go on. His legs refused to hold him and he was so hungry that he was trembling and might have fallen down in a heap right there in the middle of the street. Pushing open the iron gate of the garden, he slowly began to climb the marble stairs that led to the large outside door. He reached the door and rang the bell. The door opened slowly, she opened it. There she was standing silently in the doorway. Past middle age. Well-preserved though. And wearing a long, red velvet dressing gown and pearl earrings. He realized it was her.

"I've been waiting for you all morning," she said and took him gently by the arm to lead him into the interior of the house. "Come on in, don't be afraid."

THE HALLWAY WITH THE DARK RED RUG led to a large living room filled with old furniture and paintings. The mysterious lady and our friend were standing in front of the unlit fireplace. "What do you think of it?" she asked with a sweet, sly smile. She was fully aware that her guest was dazzled. In fact, he was flabbergasted. This house was a palace. She indicated a velvet armchair and told him that he might sit down if he liked. He looked at his clothes: they were too dirty for him to sit down in these chairs. "Sit down!" the mysterious lady who had read his thoughts urged him tenderly. — He had to sit down, they had so much to say. Marcus, however, hesitated. He was afraid that if he soiled the armchairs, she would become angry and throw him out. "Sit down, don't be afraid," she repeated with almost maternal affection. Marcus was about to sit down when his strength gave way. He lost consciousness and fell in a heap on the floor.

THE DREAM AND MEMORIES OF OUR HERO from within the sweet sensation of fainting resembled a badly made black and white film — a black and white silent film projected on an uneven white wall by an old projector. He saw himself at a younger age, wearing a white shirt and black trousers, inside the bedroom of a rustic doll's house. He saw himself full of anger, excited, frantic, shouting and kicking the tiny furniture and banging his head against the walls. As if he wanted to get away from there and was looking for a pretext to turn his back forever on all that he was living. Before him a young woman with braids was weeping and wailing, trying to stammer something through her tears. Marcus wanted to get away from that tiny house. He wanted to spread his wings, to see the world. The young woman, however, stood before him, barring his way. He told her to move away from the door and let him pass, but she insisted on standing there. Marcus rushed forward, grabbed her and threw her to the floor. He tried to leave, to go out into the world never to return to the wretchedness and orderliness inside there, but the young woman lunged and grabbed his leg. He shouted to her to let go of him and started dragging her along with him on the floor, but she clung to him and refused to release him. It was then that he took a jackknife from his pocket and threatened to cut her throat. The young woman was crying and begging him to remain inside there, in their little corner. Blinded by anger, his mind thick with smoke and plunged into darkness, Marcus slowly lowered the knife to his wife's neck. Everything happened very slowly, without a sound, with the light flickering.

HE WOKE UP THE NEXT DAY AT NOON with the mistress of the house standing over him. She was wearing an all-white silk dress. He was still lying on the rug in the large living room as he heard her telling him that it was time to wake up, he had slept long enough, it was nearly noon. At first he thought he was dreaming, but as soon as he remembered where he was he started and shrank away from her. The mysterious lady, however, was perfectly in control of the situation. "Don't get so excited," she said sweetly. "Have you forgotten where you are?" She asked him to forgive her for not moving him to a bed—he was too heavy for her—and hoped that he wasn't stiff from spending the entire night on the rug. Anxious to become indispensable to her,

Marcus took her hand with an insinuating look, but she scolded him like a small child getting into his daily mischief. — He mustn't be a bad boy. Marcus, however, wanting to prove to her that he was still of some use despite her reproaches, would not let go of her hand and began to bestow on it small hesitant kisses of a slightly passionate nature. The mysterious lady was terrified and tried to pull her hand away by force. — He mustn't do things like that, it was hardly the moment, she said to him sternly. But he had no intention of letting go of her hand. The mysterious lady made a joke of it, laughing in a manner that took the wind out of his sails and discouraged him. — It was time for him to get up from that cursed rug, to take a bath and to stop being so impetuous for no reason at all. Marcus obeyed and stood up.

What was this woman after? What did she want from him? Why was she being so nice to him? — First of all he must take a long bath, and afterwards they must sit down and have something to eat. She led him to an enormous, pure white bathroom with mirrors and marble. The bathtub was full of foam and all around it were multi-colored bottles of perfume, jars of cosmetics and earthen baskets filled with sweet smelling small bars of soap. Marcus stood staring all around in surprise and wonder. Never before in his life had he seen such surroundings.

"Get undressed!" the mysterious lady ordered. Our friend hesitated to obey her. Realizing that he was bashful, she turned to leave the bathroom. "Make sure that you wash yourself thoroughly," she said to him when she had already reached the door. Marcus, who had never before in his life met such a thoughtful person, wanted to express his gratitude to her in his warm, well-meaning and brutal manner. He rushed at her and tried to hug and kiss her, but she disengaged herself from his grasp. — Had he taken leave of his senses? What did he think he was doing? she said rather angrily. Marcus was overcome with embarrassment. After a little when things had calmed down somewhat, she said to him, "Don't be in such a hurry, you'll pay off your debt!" When Marcus found himself alone in the bathroom, he rushed forward, seized a bottle of cologne, opened it and drank the contents down at one gulp.

THE MISTRESS OF THE HOUSE WAS SEATED in the living room turning over the pages of a magazine. Someone rang the doorbell. She put the magazine down next to the sofa, looked at her wristwatch to see if her caller was punctual for their meeting and stood up to go open the door. Before opening it, she looked through the keyhole to make sure that it was the party she was expecting. After satisfying herself that it was the right person, she unlocked the door slowly. A slender, dark-complexioned young woman entered the house, dressed very smartly and with the air of someone who had money to burn. The mistress of the house told her to come in quickly. As they were crossing the hall to go into the living room, the young woman asked her if in fact anyone had shown up. "Of course someone showed up!" the woman advanced in years replied.

"Where is he now?" the young caller asked with misgiving. — Now he was taking a bath, she replied with a wink. "Already?" the young woman exclaimed. — He had been here since yesterday evening, the mysterious lady informed her, smiling enigmatically. The young woman, who had already sat down on the sofa, jumped up. "What?" she asked with alarm. — She had heard her, the stranger had been with her since yesterday evening! — And she had remained alone all night with a total stranger? — Yes! What had she to fear? "What are you saying? Have you taken leave of your senses?" the dark-complexioned young woman demanded, ready to start screaming. — He was as limp as a rag and quite incapable of harming her, the mistress of the house replied with indifference.

The young caller was annoyed but settled herself again on the sofa and simply said, "You mustn't do things like that, Mother!" — Why not? What had she to fear? she asked calmly. "You mustn't, I'm telling you . . ." The young woman felt herself in an awkward situation, horrible things happened every day, didn't she read the newspapers?

"Nothing matters to me any more, Martha!" the mysterious lady said with tearful eyes. — If nothing mattered to her, then why had she placed that damned ad in the newspaper? the young woman asked, thinking that the question would help set the old lady back on her feet psychologically. "I'm not sure why!" she replied and sat down silently in an armchair while looking sadly through the window at the trees in the garden.

"What's he like?" the young woman asked to break the silence.

"Tired and desperate!" she replied. — That's not what she meant. — Then what did she mean? The mysterious lady looked at her strangely. — She meant what's he like physically! Was he fair? Dark? Short? Tall? Average height? the young woman asked trying to be more specific. "Is that what interests you?" the mistress of the house rebuked her.

"I'm the one who's going to be saddled with him!" the young woman replied with cynicism.

"Dark and of average height. You go well together!" the older woman replied with the same cynicism.

Suddenly a frightful crash was heard that came from the bathroom, as if all the bottles of perfume had broken. The two women jumped up. What was that? Something must have broken. Filled with apprehension, they ran in the direction of the bathroom, hoping that nothing serious had happened to their guest.

THAT AFTERNOON FOUND THEM SEATED around the table in the spacious, luminous kitchen. The table was laden with porcelain, lace and lots of silver. The coffee was steaming. There were big dishes filled with sweets, cookies, croissants, fruit and other good things. Our friend was freshly bathed and wearing a snow-white, thick terry cloth robe. He was finally eating his elaborate breakfast very attentively and a little fearfully. There were tastes on that table that he was savoring for the first time in his life. The mysterious lady and the dark-complexioned Martha had finished their breakfast and were observing him out of the corner of their eye. "When are we going to hear your voice?" Martha provoked him just like that. Our friend looked at her carefully without saying anything.

This gal isn't at home with silver, lace and porcelain, he thought to himself. The mistress of the house, to surmount the awkward situation which had been created, asked her guest, for no reason, out of pure curiosity, what he had done with that entire bottle of cologne that she had found empty, had he poured it over himself or had he spilt it? Marcus raised his head and looked them both in the eye, these sly bitches noticed everything, nothing escaped them. "I drank it!" he blurted out. Neither one was expecting such an answer. Even our friend who had committed the small sin with the cologne could not believe that he actually had done it. The young caller's face became lined with dismay and in a voice filled with apprehension she said to the mistress of the house:

"He drank it, Mother!"

"Yes, I drank it!" Marcus, who had taken a dislike to this hussy from the start, repeated rather angrily. The mistress of the house asked politely if he was in the habit of taking a drink from time to time. —Sometimes, when he had worries, he replied. Martha, that is the young woman who wanted to send him packing from inside there the sooner the better, called him an alcoholic without the flicker of a doubt. The mistress of the house, however, responded indirectly to her malice by informing Marcus that she too enjoyed taking a nip from time to time.

"You're not in the habit of drinking cologne!" the young woman, who did not care one bit for the sympathy the old lady was showing this scum, tossed at her maliciously. The mistress of the house took hold of Marcus' hand with tenderness and assured him that the two of them were going to get along just fine.

Our friend, who again misinterpreted the old lady's intentions, looked deeply into her eyes and murmured a heartfelt "right!" fraught with innuendoes. Then he took away his hand and went on with his endless breakfast.

Martha, however, who all this time was on pins and needles, was again unable to restrain herself. "He frightens me, Mother!" she turned and said to the old lady, ready to start crying and to go into her usual hysterics. The mistress of the house cautioned her to control herself, it wasn't polite to say such things in front of their guest. Our friend who felt the jab was vexed.

"Who frightens her? Me?" he asked with petulance and irony.

"Yes, you!" the young woman hurled in his face, hoping to infuriate him so that he would show himself in his true colors. But he was not an inexperienced child. Realizing right away what the catty creature was after, he decided to break her nerves by pursuing another tactic.

Marcus stared into her eyes and asked her with simpleminded innocence to explain for what reason she felt this way toward him. Martha who by now was furious responded by leaning over and shouting in his face that he should ask himself that question, not her. Our friend, annoyed by the volume of her voice, dropped his head and pretended to be sad, the cologne had made him sick, justifying in this way his retreat before this frantic female. The young woman, however, refused to give up. She seemed to be choking as she watched our friend eat, crossed herself and behaved like a madwoman, repeating that this scoundrel was making her anxious. "I'll also make you happy, just give me time to get accustomed!" Marcus mocked her. The mistress of the house asked the young woman to stop pressuring their guest, because he really seemed like a very nice boy.

Our friend decided that he would get back at this bitch who was lording it over him. He decided, that is, to ask her something which had kept popping into his head all this time and which he knew perfectly well it was forbidden to ask. "Is she your daughter?" he inquired of the old lady, designating Martha with his head.

"No!" the mistress of the house replied with tearful eyes.

"What, then?" our friend plunged the knife deeper.

"Martha here is my son's fiancée!" the old lady finally made the introductions in a voice that trembled.

Martha, who had finally found her master, felt

that she was drowning in tears, she jumped up and crying disappeared into one of the rooms of the endless house. The mistress of the house stood up and ran after her to calm her down. "Martha, Martha, my girl . . . Martha, my child, be patient!" she called out sweetly as she tried to catch up with her.

Marcus had remained all alone in the kitchen. The newspaper ad had said that the woman who was looking for company was one person, yet he had found two. Strange goings-on. Something was brewing in there, only he couldn't figure out what. There was plenty of time for him to get to the bottom of things. Meanwhile he would do well to forget all that and finish his breakfast. He hadn't eaten in four days.

IN ONE OF THE BEDROOMS OF THE HOUSE young Martha and the mysterious old lady had opened a large, walnut wardrobe and were removing all sorts of men's clothes from it. After carefully examining the clothes as they held up the hangers on which they were suspended, they would spread them out painstakingly on the wide, wooden bed. Young Martha was fuming as she laid a white, silk shirt on the bed. She was speaking with firmness to the mistress of the house, telling her how surprised she was at her. —For goodness sake didn't she realize that her guest was a murderer? Hadn't she seen the dreadful tattoo on his arm? The mysterious lady, who was laying a pair of black corduroys on the bed, tried to restore her confidence. —She mustn't worry in the least, their guest was above all a very frightened individual who would not object to anything. Just as young Martha was laying an athletic sweater and a pair of briefs on the bed she burst into sobs. "Mother, I swear to you that I won't be able to love him!" she kept repeating, her eyes blurred with tears, to the mistress of the house. Holding a gray sweater made of fine wool and in an icy voice which brooked no objections, the old lady comforted her by telling her that once she got to know him better, she was bound to come to like him. —But he was an illiterate who drank cologne, hadn't she noticed the way he talked? Martha continued to object as she laid a pair of woolen socks on the bed.

The old lady bent over to place a pair of shoes next to the bed. After she straightened up again, she informed her young protégé that it didn't matter if he was illiterate. But the dark-complexioned Martha refused to beat a retreat. —The best thing for them to do was to send him away and wait for someone else to come along—someone more courteous. The old lady, however, told her in plain words that she had taken a liking to him and that she was

convinced they would never find anyone more qual-
ified than him for their experiment. His clothes on
the bed were all ready. They counted them,
recounted them, nothing was missing. As they
looked at the clothes spread out on the bed, they
fell silent. An imperceptible sadness on the verge of
becoming an emotion had taken their speech away.

The door of the room opened and their swarthy
guest entered still clad in the white terry cloth robe
he was wearing in the morning. "What's going on
here?" he asked with curiosity and perplexity. It
was obvious that he had searched half the house to
ferret them out.

"We're getting your clothes ready!" Martha
replied curtly, indicating with her head the gar-
ments that were spread out on the thick mattress.

"When did you buy them?" was all that our
friend, who for some unexplainable reason had
begun to dislike this whole situation, could find to
say.

"We didn't buy them!" Martha tossed at him,
waiting for the old lady to provide him with the
final explanation.

"They belonged to my son!" she informed him in
a voice that trembled.

"Aren't you going to get dressed?" Martha, who
had begun to savor his fear, asked concealing her
joy. Our friend Marcus, however, who was not a
man to be trifled with, cast off his terry cloth robe

and remained naked in front of them. The two women looked away.

LATE THAT SAME DAY, TOWARD EVENING, the mistress of the house led Marcus to his room. Dressed in new, clean clothes, our swarthy friend looked like another person. When they entered the huge room with the oak bookcase, the very expensive rugs and the old, gold inlaid desk, our friend had already began to have second thoughts. Quite frankly, what was he getting himself into? What did this mysterious old lady want from him? All this wealth and luxury so unexpectedly? "This will be your room!" the venerable lady said turning on a large corner lamp with a shade that gave off a sweet, honey-colored light, for outside it had already started to grow dark. The moment the room was illuminated it appeared even more imposing.

"What a lot of books, my good woman!" our friend stammered, looking with astonishment and horror at the endless rows of books in the bookcase as if to say: "What a heavy burden for any man to bear, my good woman!" The old lady, who was admiring him in his new clothes, barely heard what he said. She merely asked if the new clothes she had given him fit well. — They were a perfect fit, you might have thought she knew his size, our friend assured her. She then grabbed him by the hand, as if intoxicated, pushed open a door and led him into an adjoining room. It was the bedroom in which he had dressed that morning. She stood before a wardrobe which took up practically an entire wall and opened it wide. The wardrobe was full of clothes and they were all his, she told him with tearful eyes while caressing the clothes with her hand. "Right!" said our perplexed friend who still had not figured out what exactly was going on in this household.

Afterwards they both remained silent, not knowing how to continue their conversation. The old lady, however, who was more versed in such impasses, asked if he had any questions. "When do I get time off?" our friend, who thought he had been hired as a servant, a gardener or in some similar capacity, asked bluntly. The old lady, not expecting such an innocent question, was taken aback and felt the urge to laugh. — He could have time off whenever he liked, she informed him with a smile. Our friend didn't quite get it. The venerable lady saw that he was struggling to understand and promised that she would even give him a key of his own. At this point Marcus was at a complete loss as to what was going on. "And what am I going to do in here, be the chauffeur?" he stammered completely in the dark. — No, he wasn't going to be the chauffeur, he was simply going to live with them, the old lady informed him gently, unable to refrain from smiling.

Marcus again misinterpreted her words and approached her with naughty intentions. "Are we going to live together?" he asked as he tried to take her in his arms. The mistress of the house pushed him away with tact; this little man amused her beyond imagination with his erotic urges. — They were going to live together under the same roof, only apart, each in his own room. "What about money?" Marcus came straight to the point.

"I'll give you pocket money!" the old lady answered hastily. Our friend thought she was doing all this to make him more excited. He had heard say that rich women won't give their angel so much as a glass of water without first taking his "family jewels." Pocket money, he thought, that's crazy! and without another word he grabbed the old lady and threw her on the bed. The mistress of the house realized that she was living a tragicomic moment and attempted to resist with a certain amount of grace so as not to ruffle this tender brute too much. "Let me go!" she said struggling to get out of his frightful embrace. "What comes over you?" she asked shifting her legs in despair. "What comes over you suddenly and makes you so violent?" Marcus, however, meant mischief, he was groaning and groping his way to kiss her.

Oh my God, he had mistaken her intentions, she

had to do something. This dark barbarian would not heed her pleas to come to his senses and to control himself. "I go for you," he was moaning from on top of her while trying to kiss her. The old lady was completely flustered by all these ungraceful gymnastics and to escape once and for all from this unexpected adventure she gave him a tender smack on his flushed cheek. Marcus, highly offended, was thrown off balance and drew back. "What do you think you're doing!" he shouted in her face like a dog that had been beaten.

"There was no other way," she replied with charm while trying to reconstruct her social image.

"I don't get this game!" he hummed and hawed, his eyes drowned in sorrow and hatred by the provocation. The mistress of the house had finally managed to get up from the bed. She straightened her disheveled dress as best she could, arranged her hair, stood before him and decided to clear up this question of lovemaking once and for all. —He should listen here, these shenanigans were not for her. It was too late for that. If he wanted a woman, he could go after Martha. Our friend received the idea enthusiastically.

THE NEXT DAY THE MISTRESS OF THE HOUSE decided to send Marcus and Martha on a stroll through the shops to enable them to become better acquainted. All the while they were walking and buying things, however, they did not talk to each other. At some point toward noon when, weighed down with packages, they both felt like sitting down in a pastry shop and having a drink of cold water, they were forced under the circumstances to converse.

"What happened?" asked Martha, who had opened her handbag and was touching up her make-up.

"What do you think happened? Nothing at all!" our friend replied glumly. Afterwards she changed the subject and asked him what he was going to order. —He hadn't made up his mind yet. Martha was annoyed that he was unwilling to enter into a conversation with her and told him that he could do whatever he liked but to leave her alone.

"I don't get this game!" Marcus suddenly blurted out. Martha was taken aback. She put down her lipstick and hand-mirror and looked into his eyes. —What game was he talking about? "The game!" he repeated monosyllabically. Martha pretended not to understand. —Whatever did he mean, what game? —The one they were playing behind his back. —If he made a slight effort, he'd also understand something about life, Martha replied ironically and picked up her hand-mirror and lipstick to finish painting her lips.

"Does she have money?" our friend went on with

his interrogation, ignoring the jabs of this ninny who was acting the grand lady with him. —Did who have money? she asked looking at him out of the corner of her hand-mirror because she did not like the tone of his voice. "The lady!" he replied. —The lady in question had more money than he could ever imagine. —Then what in hell did she want from him, a former convict? —If she told him exactly what it was that she wanted from him, he would take to his heels, Martha replied, adjusting one of her eyelashes. He squeezed her hand and assured her that things like that didn't frighten him. Martha pulled away and cautioned him to keep quiet for she had just seen the old lady walking toward them, smiling. She was dressed in a grey suit and had a bouquet of carnations in her hands. Thinking that the ice between them had been broken, she was pleased to see Marcus holding Martha's hand.

"You two seem to have a lot to talk about!" she said gleefully as she pulled up a chair and sat down beside them. The venerable lady was surprised that they had not ordered anything. —The waiter had forgotten them, Martha mumbled as she arranged her cosmetics in her handbag. "Waiter! Waiter!" the old lady shouted all ready to order something spectacular to celebrate their first outing.

THAT SAME DAY EARLY IN THE AFTERNOON Marcus and Martha were seated on a bench with all their packages next to them. In a manner that brooked no objection the mysterious lady had advised them to stay there and wait for her. She had an errand to do but would not be long. "Where did she go?" our friend asked the young woman brusquely.

"To the bridge!" she replied without turning to look at him. —What bridge and nonsense was this bitch talking about? —Today was the anniversary and she was going to the bridge.

"Bridge? Anniversary?" Marcus understood nothing; this harlot was making fun of him. —It wasn't her fault if he was thickheaded. Anyway it would be better if the old lady herself explained to him, Martha concluded, anxious to change the subject.

That did it! These strange women were putting him through hoops, they were all mystery and intrigue, they wanted to drive him mad. He jumped up and grabbed her by the shoulders. "Speak! Goddamn it! Speak!" he shouted in her face. Martha tried to protest. —If he didn't leave her alone she'd scream. Without releasing his grip on her, he extended his thumbs to her neck. "Speak!" he said through clenched teeth. Martha was frightened out of her mind.

"Leave me alone, you pig!" she said sobbing and

writing with pain. "Leave me alone, you criminal! You murderer! I'll scream!" But there was no way she could free herself from his iron palms. Marcus, his face gray and petrified, started to squeeze her neck.

"Speak, goddamn it! Speak!" he kept repeating mechanically, as if begging her to speak before something terrible happened. The young woman was terrified. She realized that our young friend was not joking, if she delayed even the slightest this murderer would choke her.

"Her son, her son," she stammered gasping for breath, "killed himself. He fell in front of a train . . . from the bridge!"

—Good, now that she had told him, why didn't he leave her neck alone? Didn't he realize he was hurting her? Marcus took his hands off her and remained staring at her in silence, as if the attempt at murder had paralyzed his body. To allow him time to regain his self-possession and while rubbing her neck, Martha reeled off more things. "The lady's son was sick! He didn't want to live! He loved no one, that's why he killed himself!"

TOWARD LATE AFTERNOON THAT SAME DAY the old lady, her eyes full of emotion, approached the bench where Marcus and Martha were seated, slowly and like a sorrowful sleepwalker. When she saw them that way, withdrawn into themselves, like two petrified birds, she felt like teasing them a little. "What's going on?" she asked smiling bitterly. "Have you finally come to love one another?"

"We're trying!" her protégé snapped back at her, seething with anger that she had forced her to remain waiting all this time next to such a coarse individual. The old lady pretended not to have heard and tried to change the subject, telling them that she had finished her errand and that if they liked they could all return home together at last. Neither Martha, nor Marcus stirred from their seats.

"Who does the room I'm occupying belong to?" our friend, his face somber, asked, hoping to unravel this entire mystery right then and there. The old lady did not seem startled by his crude, abrupt manner and reacted as if expecting such behavior on his part. She reminded him that she had already told him. —The room he was occupying belonged to her son. —And where was her son now? our friend went on with his awkward interrogation, hoping to gather enough information to know which of the two women was lying.

"He's abroad studying!" the rich lady replied with complete naturalness. The blood rushed to his head. This woman lied the way she breathed. He felt the urge to strike her but controlled himself.

"Abroad? Is that what the cemetery's called?" he asked his eyes flaming. At first she acted as if she didn't understand what he was talking about, but after a few moments she reversed herself and her eyes filled with tears. So her protégé had given him a complete report. Martha, fearing the consequences, tried to justify herself by claiming that he had hit her, that he had almost strangled her, that he had nearly broken her arm.

The old lady set her at ease. —She had done well to tell him. It didn't upset her in the least. He should know too. Afterwards she turned to our friend and began to speak about her son with deep emotion. She told him that her son was extremely handsome, that he excelled in everything, in his studies, in dance—in everything. He was also very athletic. But that in the last analysis he was unable to go on living. At least that's what he wrote in the letter they found in his desk. Her son was unable to go on living and went and threw himself on the train tracks. Even Martha, with whom he had enjoyed a close relationship for years, had not been able to keep him alive. She did not know what exactly had happened. Her son had everything, he lacked nothing. Now she came to the bridge every year on the day the terrible event occurred and threw a bouquet of red carnations on the tracks. It was impossible for her to continue, sorrow, like an unliftable weight, was pressing down on her bosom.

She dropped her head and remained silent. "I didn't see any photographs in the house!" our friend muttered slowly. The old lady tossed back her head abruptly, her face blazing with anger and malice.

"I burned them all!" she replied coldly.

THAT SAME DAY AT DUSK, ALL THREE OF THEM went to the cemetery to visit his grave. It was a large monument, near the entrance, at the very front. Next to the candle, inside a small marble iconostasis, was his picture. "That's him!" his mother said taking the picture in her hands. Marcus asked her to hand him the picture because it had gotten dark and he couldn't see very well. The old lady had no objection.

"He was a good-looking young man!" Marcus murmured examining the picture.

"But you haven't told us anything about yourself!" the rich lady broached the subject delicately as she took her son's picture and returned it to its place next to the snuffed out candle.

"What can I say?" Marcus stammered uneasily. —First of all they didn't even know his name. — Yes, what was his name? Martha, who was just waiting for an opportunity to put him on the spot, insisted. —He was called Marcus. Now was she satisfied?

"And why were you in jail all these years, Marcus?" asked the old lady almost simultaneously and without allowing him time to catch his breath as she cleaned the candle on her son's grave. Our friend was dumbfounded. How had this magpie found out that he had been in prison? Martha sensed what he was thinking and came to his aid. —He shouldn't take it to heart, madam knew important people, she had merely asked and been informed. —If she had asked and been informed, then why was she asking again now? our friend snarled through his teeth, about to go blind with hatred and to give free rein to his anger and, in so doing, to blow everything sky high. The old lady turned and looked at him. "I didn't ask anyone," she said. "I just knew!" Marcus looked at her with awe and immediately crawled back into his shell. At times that old woman had a gaze that brooked no objection, she could send you before the firing squad at the drop of a hat.

"That's different!" he stammered quite ready to relate the story of his life.

"Well, then?" asked the old lady who didn't like to be kept waiting.

"Well, then," our friend began. "I was born in a village. My father went off to foreign lands. When my brothers and I grew up, they unleashed us down here in the city. Now do you understand? Work from morning till night. A wretched exis-

104

tence! We were only boys and we longed for the good things in life. There was no one to hold us back and we got mixed up in crime. A few small holdups — something here, something there — and we ended up in the clink for fifteen long years. After our mother died we each went our separate ways. When they told me they were going to release me, I went to the prison warden and asked, couldn't you keep me in here a little longer, my good man, couldn't you keep me until after Christmas, because I have no one out there. That, in brief, is the story of my life, more or less."

"And what can you do?" asked the mistress of the house, hitting him where he was most vulnerable. — Lots of things and nothing, our friend replied in a sad voice.

AFTER THESE REVELATIONS the three of them went home. Marcus had stretched out on the bed and was deep in thought. He still couldn't figure out what this lady with her millions was up to. She had not been fazed in the least to learn that he had done time in jail, on the contrary she had seemed pleased. The other one though, the younger woman, had pulled a long face. Suddenly he got up and went into the next room, sat down in the desk chair and tried to figure out what his next move would be. He had searched the wardrobe, he had searched the desk drawers, he had searched everywhere. Not a thing! He hadn't found a single thing which might give him a clue. His attention was drawn to the bookcase. That had not been searched by him. He made his way over to the imposing piece of furniture, pulled out a thick book from one of the shelves and started leafing through it. Inside the pages he found a letter. He put the book down on the desk and started to open it. At that moment there was a knock on the door. He concealed the letter hastily and went to unlock the door.

Martha was standing in the opening of the door, dressed in a provocative evening dress. Her perfume made him giddy and left him speechless. She beckoned him to step aside and entered the room, then beckoned him to close the door. Marcus obeyed. He closed the door and locked it turning the key twice. "Is it really you?" he stammered dazed.

"I think we should talk!" she replied in a velvet voice.

"Sit down!" our friend, who had suddenly begun to perspire, said to her.

"Lock the door!" Martha ordered blowing the smoke from her cigarette in his face. — That wasn't necessary, he had already locked it. — The old lady was in the dining room preparing a special meal, she said and winked at him. Marcus, misunderstanding her intentions, thought she was asking him in a roundabout way to make love to her; there was plenty of time for that. He went up to her, therefore, and whispered softly in her ear that he was glad the old lady was busy with dinner. Martha became irate and decided to set things straight immediately. She pushed him aside and, looking at him ironically, informed him that the old lady was preparing the meal in order to announce their engagement.

Instead of being distressed by the news, Marcus was elated. "I like!" he exclaimed and pounced on her to snatch a kiss. But Martha, taking two small steps to the side, escaped his embrace. When she had recovered her equilibrium and felt a little more secure, she let him know in an icy tone of voice that such an engagement was not at all to her liking. "Then why don't you get up and leave!" our friend retorted as if he had carefully prepared his answer.

"Look who's giving orders," she threw in his face and turned her back to him. —In that case, he replied, if it was her intention to stay, she really ought to obey and do whatever the old lady asked of her. Martha, who did not appreciate being mocked by this scoundrel, flew into a passion. She turned abruptly and looked at him, her face crimson with rage. "Why don't you leave, you vicious dog!" she said stamping her foot on the floor.

"And go where?" he replied ironically.

"Where you came from!" Martha shouted contemptuously.

"That's not possible!" Marcus said smiling.

"Are you implying that you've taken a fancy to me?" the young woman, looking at him with disdain, sought to belittle him. — He wasn't sticking around because of her pretty eyes, it was simply that it suited him, that's all, our friend muttered, ready to burst into laughter at the expression of horror on her face. — So he had decided to stay? the young woman stammered, terrified.

"Uh-huh!" Marcus finished her off with one word. — But the old lady was stark-raving mad, didn't he realize what he was getting himself into by staying there? Martha sought to unnerve him.

"I'm used to desperate situations!" our friend cut her off abruptly.

"Then you really have made up your mind to stay?" the strange woman murmured to our friend, staring blankly at the bookcase. — They had said it for the umpteenth time. He had made up his mind to stay; she would simply have to resign herself to the fact and calm down. — The old lady wanted to keep him there in order to marry them, said Martha, hoping to terrorize him once more by announcing the plans of her mistress. — Was she saying that to frighten him? Personally he rather liked the idea. — She was only telling him because she didn't particularly care for him; in fact, she found him disgusting. — Nor did he care for her and her rotten disposition. — The old lady might marry them, but if he so much as dared lay a hand on her, he would regret it bitterly. — Who was going to prevent him? Since she was going to be his little woman in all due form. — Was it his intention to rape her?

— This gal wanted everything her own way, but life wasn't like that. — If he forced her to do something against her will — she was only telling him so he'd know from the start — it would be war between them. At this point our friend got good and mad. What war and nonsense was this nut talking about? — She knew very well that they were both powerless to do anything. The situation was perfectly clear: either she married him or she left. There was, of course, another solution. She could kill the old lady or the groom before the marriage could take place. It was in her power, but she was the one who would have to decide. She told him that he was pushing her too far and that one day she would get back at him for driving her into a corner like this.

"Did you at least love her son?" Marcus asked, hoping to give her the coup de grâce with his question. He had made a big mistake, however. The heartless creature was scarcely interested.

"I tried!" she replied with indifference.

"Did you at least help him?" our friend per-

109

sisted, his eyes becoming compassionate like those of a wounded dog. She approached the door, but before leaving the room she turned and told him to make sure that he wore a suit and tie. The dinner was to be formal.

As they stood there about to come to blows, they heard the old lady, who was trying to open the door and enter the room. When she realized it was locked, she began calling: "Where are you? Where are you? What in heaven's name is going on? Did you lock yourselves inside?" After trying several times to open the door and finally realizing that they really were locked inside, the old lady broke into peals of laughter. "Ha! Ha! Ha! Hurry up, do you hear? Ha! Ha! Ha! the soufflé will get cold!" she kept repeating as she walked down the corridor toward the interior of the house, convulsed with laughter.

BEFORE THEY SAT DOWN AT THE TABLE our friend went into the bathroom and locked the door. He wanted to read the letter he had found in the book; his curiosity was aroused. Behind him, inside the bathroom mirror, the old lady's son appeared, looking just as he did in the picture they had found on top of his grave. Our friend had his back to the wash-stand, so it was entirely impossible for him to see

110

the ghost reading the letter with his soundless lips. "You, my friend, who will find this letter, listen to what the son of this house who grew weary and ended his life before growing old has to say."

The mistress of the house, adorned with her jewelry and a formal, two-piece dress, was leaning against the bathroom door trying to open it. She was convinced that something evil was going on behind this strange door. "Marcus! Marcus!" she called out while knocking discreetly on the door. "Marcus, my boy, what are you doing in there? Have you gone mad? Come and sit down at the table!" Our friend, however, remained tongue-tied and ignored her as he went on reading the letter with the ghost behind his back.

"I had grown weary, my friend, I would look at my hands and not recognize them, I would look at my feet and not feel anything. I had grown weary!"

The old lady, however, who had lived through a similar scene once before, was out of her mind with fear. Now she was banging on the door and practically screaming with anguish. "Marcus! Marcus! Open this door! Speak to me, are you alive?" So that she might hear his voice and calm down, our friend shouted that he would be through in a minute. Then he plunged back into the letter.

"I never lived. Not as a child. Nor as a young man. Nor as a student. Even though we had a great deal of money, mother wanted me to become suc-

cessful and famous and had planned my life probably to my last breath. This is how my life went by,
my friend, in the presence of teachers and under
constant supervision. Always bent over a book!"

Even though she had heard his voice, the old
lady refused to calm down—she had lived through
this scene once before—and continued to bang on
the door, asking with anguish: "Marcus! Marcus!
What's going on? What are you doing in there?"

"I'm shaving! our friend replied. —Then why
had he locked the door? —Had he really? He wasn't
aware of it! When had he done that? —Why
wouldn't he open the door? —He couldn't, his
hands were covered with foam, he couldn't take
hold of the doorknob. The old lady seemed convinced that nothing evil was astir.

"Very well!" she stammered through her teeth
and moved away from the door. Marcus went on
reading the letter in the company of the ghost.

"I learned languages, I studied music, I earned
degrees. I turned thirty and had barely lived. One
morning I left home. Disappeared. I thought that
this would be life, that this would be freedom. I was
mistaken! Out there things were much more diffi-
cult. Mother had been right. Six months later I
returned home!"

Martha approached the bathroom door. —What
in blazes was going on in there? The old lady was
alarmed and wanted to call the police. Our friend,

112

without bothering to open the door, appealed to Martha to stop her. The young woman suddenly changed her attitude toward him and decided to do what he asked of her. She hurried away from the door and went to look for the old lady before she did anything foolish. Marcus went on reading the letter. "I went back. My adventure, however, had been inconclusive. I had not been completely convinced. My father fought for four years, after that he kept quiet. But I could see what my life was going to be like to the very end. I could see my ordeal and I was pleasureless. Nothing gave me pleasure. This is why I decided to die the sooner the better. My mother did her best to keep me here among you. She even consented to my marriage with Martha. I had picked Martha up in the street the time I had left home.

"To be continued, my friend! You will find further details in other letters that are inside the books!"

Marcus folded the letter and put it in his pocket. The silent ghost behind him emerged from the mirror and resumed his invisible form. The old lady returned to the bathroom door. This time she was slightly out of control, shouting and banging on the door as if she was having an attack of nerves. —If he did not open the door this minute, she would be forced to call the police. The door opened slowly and our friend came out safe and sound. For a moment the old lady was confused, having expected a more dramatic unfolding of events. But when she saw him emerge from the bathroom in one piece, she calmed down and made a joke of it. — What had he been doing in there all this time? He was no longer a fourteen-year-old locking himself in the bathroom for hours to read pornographic magazines. The food was getting cold. He must come quickly and sit right down at the table.

THEY WERE NOW ALL SEATED around a large table laden with crystal, silver, lighted candles, flowers and all kinds of food. The mistress of the house was deeply moved and wished to talk to him about the happiness they were about to live. Holding a crystal glass in her hand and taking a sip of red wine from time to time, she launched into her speech.

"Before we start eating, I want to tell you something, children!" the old lady began. "I want to see you happy! I want you to fill the house with children! I want my house to be alive again! Don't worry about money! I'll take care of everything! What I want is to see you happy! What I want is for you to love one another! I want life to be victorious! Love! Happiness! My son was unable to continue! God who is most merciful and who took him next to him must know something that we do not know.

This is why I try not to be sad. This is why you are going to be like children to me now! Because you have suffered and have an appetite for life. My son was used to an easy life. I did all that I could to save him but he wouldn't listen to me . . ." With tearful eyes she opened her gold-embroidered bag and took out a small velvet case. She opened it. Inside were two diamond wedding rings. "Here are your rings!" she said and presented them with them. "Put them on!"

Marcus and Martha took the diamond wedding rings and put them on.

"It is now time for us to make a wish!" the old lady exclaimed as she raised her crystal glass with the dark red wine in the air.

"To our health! And to your happiness!"

Marcus and Martha began to drink in silence. They remained motionless, as if they were not yet used to their new situation.

"I want my home to open again and to be filled with laughter and joy!" the old lady ended her toast with tearful eyes.

LATE THAT NIGHT MARCUS AND MARTHA were seated on the same bed.

"Now what?" our friend asked with embarrass-ment. Martha began to undress with slow, languorous movements. —Since the old lady had pronounced them officially engaged and wanted them to sleep together, they would do just that, it wasn't the end of the world. —So, then, she had made up her mind? our friend remarked as he unbuttoned his shirt. —Of course she had made up her mind, Martha reassured him and turned her back to him so that he could unzip her. —Seriously though, where had the old lady's son met her?

"At college, where else?" Martha replied without giving it much thought.

"Were you going down stairs?" our friend asked ironically. The young woman was taken aback, what stairs was this jerk talking about. Marcus, who in the meantime had taken off his trousers, continued to pull her leg. "I'm saying did you have to go down stairs to enter the college?" he asked again emphatically. Martha, who still didn't know what he was driving at, decided not to attach too much importance to it. —She didn't remember going down any stairs. No, she was sure of it, there were no stairs at the college, so how could she go down them? "Were there red lights?" our friend asked who was shy of taking off all his clothes.

"At Christmas when they decorated the tree there were!" replied Martha, who was now completely naked. Then she pulled back the covers and lay down on the bed. Our friend, however, preferred to put on his pajamas.

"Are you remembering the old days?" he tossed at her, looking deeply into her eyes. The young woman was baffled. — What old days? What was he trying to say, what did he mean? — He meant the clientele! our friend sneered at her, lying down in bed next to her on top of the covers. Martha changed countenance; this joker knew everything. She sat up in bed, her face deathly pale and covered with cold perspiration, and asked him how he knew. — He remembered her, our friend, who enjoyed tormenting her, snapped back. — What did he want now? she stammered. Did he intend to blackmail her? Everyone knew her secret except him. Our friend put his arms around her and started kissing her on the neck. — What he wanted was to enjoy her to the limit, like all the others. Martha gave him free rein to take his revenge without participating in the least and staring straight ahead at the molding all around the ceiling.

"I'm sick of the whole bloody lot of you, God how you disgust me . . . I wanted to remain alone with the old lady, but luck wasn't with me!" she whispered in his ear as she heard him groaning and sweating on top of her. Now he remembered her! It was Martha who always stood behind the bar. And it was at the "Black Cat." At that time they didn't ask her to sleep with the clients because she was under age. But the little girl had grown up. Yes sir, she had grown up! "You're also a murderer just

like the others. You're all murderers! Murderers!"
The woman was shouting sweetly in his ear. To
make her stop he bit her savagely on the lips.

THE DREAM AND MEMORIES OF OUR HERO from within
the sweet sensation of fainting resembled a badly
made black and white film. A black and white silent
film projected on an uneven white wall by an old
projector. He saw himself at a younger age, wearing
a white shirt and black trousers, inside the bedroom
of a village house. He saw himself full of anger,
excited, frantic, shouting and kicking the furniture
and banging his head against the walls. As if he
wanted to get away from there and was looking for
a pretext to do something that was horrible. Before
him a young woman was lying at his feet, weeping
and wailing. She was clinging to his thigh and
wouldn't let go of him. "I'm leaving! Goddamn it!"
he shouted. He wanted to bash her head in with his
fists but could not bring himself to do it.

"Where do you want to go, Marcus dear! Where
do you want to go?" She was crying and beating her
breast and would not let go of his leg for anything
in the world. "How can you abandon me like this?
Why do you want to leave? Why, why won't you
stay here? Where do you want to go?" He wanted to
strike her but could not, because he loved her. All

he could do was to cry heartrendingly and tell her to shut up. She refused to listen to him and was assailed by a feeling of injustice: he was going to throw away his life. "No, no, I'll scream, I won't let you leave! I won't let you be destroyed by the world," she said blinded by tears. "I'll call my brothers and they'll keep you here!" she threatened.

Marcus was shaking his leg in an attempt to free himself. He rushed toward the door but she was barring his way. "Get away from the door!" he yelled. "Get away from the door or I'll hit you!" She refused to budge and told him that he could hit her as much as he liked, but that she wouldn't get out of the way. He pushed her and threw her on the floor, but she sprang up and grabbed him by the waist.

"No, no," she screamed, "I won't let you leave! I won't let you destroy yourself!" He started to leave but she clung to him and he dragged her behind him as he headed for the door. He threatened to kill her if she didn't let go of him, to hit her, to bash her head in.

"I'm drowning, I'm lost in here, I'll go mad!" he shouted, crying and trying to wrest himself free from his wife. She was becoming an encumbrance, she was getting entangled in his feet. She was bringing him to his knees, keeping him in the house.

"No, no, you're going to stay here!" she said crying plaintively. "Here . . . together with your wife. We're going to have children," she said. "We're going to succeed in life!"

He took his jackknife from his pocket, opened it and brought it next to her white neck. "I'm drowning, woman, I'm drowning!" he said and he was crying like a small child. "I'll kill you! I'll go mad if I remain locked up in here! Let me leave or I'll kill you!" Afterwards the blood fell in his eyes and blinded him. Then he woke up, terrified. He was in this luxurious house, asleep in the bed of the son who committed suicide. Next to him, the beautiful woman was breathing deeply from within her satiated and undisturbed sleep.

This was the second time he had remembered and had this dream since coming to this house. In prison he had forgotten all those things. He climbed out of bed like a sleepwalker and went to find the old lady in her room.

HE OPENED THE DOOR SLOWLY AND ENTERED THE ROOM. The old lady, who had not yet gone to sleep, was sitting on her bed, reading a book. She had known he would come and had been waiting for him. Our friend advanced toward her slowly, as if hypnotized. "I know that you killed your wife!" the mis-

120

tress of the house said to him calmly and simply. Marcus stopped short as if he had been punched in the chest. — She had inquired and been told everything about him. In the courtroom he had alleged that his wife was cheating on him, but it wasn't true. Our friend once again slowly started to move toward her. — He wanted to leave his home, to abandon his wife, but she wouldn't let him. That was the reason why he killed her. Our friend was now standing quite close to her. "You were restless at home! You wanted to go out! But she wouldn't let you!" The old lady continued to provoke him. "You killed her and you paid for it!" Our friend was now next to her, he sat down gently on the bed. "I . . . I'm going to offer you one last chance," she said serenely. He reached out with his hands and grabbed her by the neck. "You're no longer young, you're hardly up to things like that any more!" she continued calmly and quietly. He hesitated, unable to squeeze her neck with his hands. "You're lucky to have met me!" His hands refused to obey him. "You must resign yourself!" Marcus, his hands around the old lady's neck, burst into angry tears. "That's how life is! There is no liberty out there where you want to go! Only hunger, disease and loneliness lying in wait for you," the old lady sought to console him.

121

WHEN MARTHA WOKE UP AND DID NOT FIND the "murderer" asleep next to her, she became alarmed. She leaped out of bed, slipped into a nightdress and began to search the rooms of the house one by one. When she entered her mistress' bedroom and beheld the spectacle on the bed, she started screaming and calling for help. In fact she headed for the telephone to call the police, but the old lady ordered her to remain calm. — Marcus wasn't going to harm her. He had come to a decision. Marcus was now her man.

Poor Martha did not know what to do. How could she remain calm when she could see the murderer's paws clasped around her mistress' neck. He was going to strangle her, that was the one certainty. Her mistress, however, was not afraid in the least. "Gently, Martha!" she whispered slowly. "Marcus wants to live! He wants to come over to our side! He won't harm me!"

— But that criminal was squeezing her neck, he intended to kill her.

— He had no such intention! the old lady murmured as she took our friend's hands and placed them gently on the bed. Afterwards she hugged his head, deeply moved.

"He's made up his mind! He's made up his mind!" Martha said crying.

"He's going to remain here with us. You'll see,

Martha! You'll see! We're all going to live together happily!"

Our friend slowly slipped from the bed and fell to the floor. He kneeled on the rug, buried his face in his hands and burst into sobs.

"Life has triumphed, my girl! Life has triumphed, Martha!" the mistress of the house kept saying amidst tears of happiness and joy.

In the mirror, however, which was over the night table next to the large bed of the old lady, the dead son's ghost had appeared. He had something he wanted to tell us.

"And so they lived happily ever after!" he said. "The mother may have won this round, but things aren't that simple! We'll talk about it again, you can be sure of that!" he concluded with a bitter smile. Afterwards he winked at us slyly, and then, as was only natural, he disappeared into the cold surface of the mirror.

GIORGOS MANIOTIS

One of the best-known young playwrights, Giorgos Maniotis was born in Athens in 1951. He studied Law in Salonica. His plays include: *The Football Match, Common Sense, Pit of Sin, The Spouses, Sedentary Life, Order and Disorder.* In recent years, he has turned to other forms of prose: *The Unknown Soldier*, a mystery novelette. *Black Tales*, tales for grown-ups. *Terrible Protection*, novel. *Winter Repertory*, thriller. *The Sly Path*, novel. *Springtime Repertory*, thriller.

NICHOLAS KOSTIS

Nicholas Kostis is a professor at Boston University where he teaches French literature and a course on French film. In addition to essays on Stendhal, Baudelaire, Apollinaire, Proust and Evelyn Waugh, he is the author of *The Exorcism of Sex and Death in Julien Green's Novels* and two books of translations, *Modern Greek Short Stories* and *Poems* by Dinos Christianopoulos. He has also published criticism on Kostas Taktsis. Nicholas Kostis is of Greek descent.

LIST OF TITLES IN
THE "MODERN GREEK WRITERS" SERIES

GIORGOS HEIMONAS *The Builders*
Novel. Translated by Robert Crist

YORGOS IOANNOU *Good Friday Vigil*
Short Stories. Translated by Peter Mackridge and Jackie Willcox

IAKOVOS KAMBANELLIS *Mauthausen*
Chronicle. Translated by Gail Holst-Warhaft

ALEXANDROS KOTZIAS *Jaguar*
Novel. Translated by H.E. Criton

MENIS KOUMANDAREAS *Koula*
Novel. Translated by Kay Cicellis

MARGARITA LIBERAKI *Three Summers*
Novel. Translated by Karen Van Dyck

GIORGOS MANIOTIS *Two Thrillers*
Translated by Nicholas Kostis

CHRISTOFOROS MILIONIS *Kalamás and Achéron*
Short Stories. Translated by Marjorie Chambers

COSTOULA MITROPOULOU *The Old Curiosity Shop on Tsimiski Street*
Novel. Translated by Elly Petrides

KOSTAS MOURSELAS *Red Dyed Hair*
Novel. Translated by Fred A. Reed

ARISTOTELIS NIKOLAIDIS *Vanishing-point*
Novel. Translated by John Leatham

ALEXIS PANSELINOS *Betsy Lost*
Novel. Translated by Caroline Harbouri

SPYROS PLASKOVITIS   *The Façade Lady of Corfu*
Novel.   Translated by Amy Mims

VANGELIS RAPTOPOULOS   *The Cicadas*
Novel.   Translated by Fred A. Reed

YANNIS RITSOS   *Iconostasis of Anonymous Saints*
Novel (?)   Translated by Amy Mims

ARIS SFAKIANAKIS   *The Emptiness Beyond*
Novel.   Translated by Caroline Harbouri

DIDO SOTIRIOU   *Farewell Anatolia*
Novel.   Translated by Fred A. Reed

STRATIS TSIRKAS   *Drifting Cities*
A Trilogy.   Translated by Kay Cicellis

ALKI ZEI   *Achilles' fiancée*
Novel.   Translated by Gail Holst-Warhaft